the BOARPIT

Alexandra Iff

*To the ones who crave too much - and refuse to
apologize for it.*

CONTENTS

AUTHOR'S NOTE

The BOARPIT is Book 1 in the Miami Ruthless series. It's a dark mafia reverse harem romance that explores mature themes, including scenes of dubious consent, violence, and sexual content, which may be triggering for some readers.

<h1 style="text-align:center">CHAPTER 1</h1>

<h2 style="text-align:center">RIO</h2>

Fucking assholes.

That bomb was meant for both of us, but it was Brox, my brother, who nearly paid the price. I pace the length of my office like a caged animal, my hand clenching around a cigarette I shouldn't even be smoking.

"Do they know," I hiss, "I will skin them alive if by any fucking chance I find out it's the Puccinis?"

"Rio," Sol, Brox's right-hand man, is trying to reign in my anger. He's standing across the room, six-foot-two, steroid-pumped arms. "You got to calm down. We know nothing about the bomb or who dropped it. The delivery company said their truck was stolen," he says, bracing for a blow.

Brox got knocked out in the explosion, but it wasn't anything serious. Still, I made him stay at the penthouse for the past few days. With Brox being at home, Sol is now acting as my new Head of Security. And he knows I'm prone to outbursts that cost people's lives. In all the years he's been with us, he's seen us do the most gruesome things men could possibly do. All thanks to my foster father, Valentino, who made us into who we are today– Satan incarnate.

"You think I give a shit about the delivery company?" I stub the cigarette into the ashtray and start pacing again. "You know what I did to their CEO?"

Sol doesn't answer. Smart.

"He's dead. That fucker isn't breathing anymore."

"You didn't actually–"

"Don't finish that sentence, Sol. Don't insult me with your shocked morality." I stop pacing and stare him down. "You think I'd let a man walk free after seeing his van deliver a bomb to my place of work?"

"You're under a microscope right now, Rio. We all are." He's always trying to tame me, to be the sanity behind my madness.

But it only makes me laugh. "Good. Let them watch. Let the whole goddamn world see what happens when you go after what's mine."

"Brox needs you stable. Not like this."

"Don't you dare tell me what Brox needs," my voice drops to a whisper. "You think this is unstable? This is mercy. If I snapped, I'd burn Key Biscayne to the ground and serve the ashes to the fucking Puccinis."

"What about the club?" Sol tries to get to me. "Now that we have no pets... I mean, with the bomb exploding, everyone ran away and we're still searching. The Boarpit can't run by itself, you know. We need– "

"Then get better at running it," I snarl. "You're head of security now, Sol. Act like it."

He shifts like he wants to argue. "Is Brox at the penthouse right now?"

"Where the fuck else would he be?"

"I'm gonna check on him."

"Do whatever you want. Go jerk off in a corner for all I care."

He nods once, without meeting my eyes. "Okay. I'll head out."

"Go."

The door shuts behind him, and I'm alone again with my rage.

I sit at my desk. The laptop glows at me like it holds answers. It doesn't. Not yet. But it will.

I'll find out who did this. Who ordered it. Who stood by and watched. And then I'll barbecue them slowly.

Brox. My brother. My only fucking family.

I swore he'd never face the Armageddon of emotions that tore through me when we lost our parents, yet I failed him. Me, the one who controls everything, who bends the world to my will. From the hell of a foster home to the heights of Miami's dark elite, we've been inseparable. We built this together. Crawled through blood, betrayal, and backroom deals to forge the Boarpit, our empire, our monument to power. And now, because some greedy little cockroaches want our kingdom, they think killing us will be enough? Fuck that.

The Puccinis have been sniffing around Fisher and Palm Island for months, their greasy fingers trying to worm into every bar and back alley. Now they want a piece of Key Biscayne. They want my streets. My money. My people. If I have to guess who did this, it would be them.

BROX

The elevator doors slide open, and I catch the almost soundless tread of someone slipping inside.

I'm in my living room, away from the elevator. One has to walk through a set of double glass doors to get to the inside of my penthouse, and to me.

"Who's there?"

My finger's already on the trigger. Safety's off. I'm ready. Hell, I'm always ready these days. But then it hits me first, his cologne. Overpowering. "Sol? That you?"

"It's me, yeah." As soon as he appears he sees my gun pointing in his direction. "Oh fuck, Brox, you got a gun!"

"And your point is?" he should know by now not to mess with me.

"Just... put it away. Please."

I cock the gun again, fast, just to hear him flinch. Just to remind him I may have been knocked out, but I'm still me. Still Brox fucking Boar. "I'll do what I want."

He knows boars can kill you without even trying to. I've done it before. Lucky strikes, Rio and I call them. Like that one time when the police captain was just about to pull his gun on us, and Rio's gun fired all by itself. Killed dead that mother fucker.

I fire at the ceiling. The shot ricochets in the room. Dust rains. Somewhere inside the penthouse, Greta screams.

"She's tidying up," I let out a dry laugh. "Better warn her next time."

"What do you want, Sol?" I finally ask.

"I thought I'd find peace here, but I see you're as crazy as your brother."

"Glad you got that cleared up."

"When are you coming back to work?" I think he came for this information.

"Tonight."

"See you at the club, then." Sol's shoes echo as he leaves. The sound of the elevator doors sliding twice tells me I'm alone again.

I leave my gun on the armrest, my other hand lands over my cell. The blast rips through my thoughts, not as trauma, but as opportunity.

Maybe now, with the Black Chamber's pets scattered like rats, Rio will finally see my point. If we want to grow as a cartel, we need to enter other markets, guns, drugs, something with reach.

Keeping pets and filming them with Miami's elite has brought us good time, money, and leverage... but all our eggs in one basket? That's suicide.

This bomb proved it. One hit, and everyone slipped through our fingers.

My cell buzzes, pulling me out of the thoughts. I swipe to answer.

"Yeah."

Rio's annoyed voice crackles through the line. "Brox."

"Rio." I lean my head back. "What now?"

He doesn't answer right away. That pause? It's his anger. I know him. He's in the office right now, leaning on that black marble desk, overlooking the club below.

"Someone's coming to see you."

"What for?"

"Guess, you idiot!" he growls. "I got the hospital to send someone to check up on you."

"Rio, no." I fucking hate doctors. "I'm fine. Seriously. I'm working tonight, anyway."

"You've hardly seen anyone. Stop being so fucking scared," he snaps.

My jaw clenches, hard enough to hurt. "Why don't you come here, I'll show you how scared I am!"

I cut the line and put the cell down. I've had enough of this crap. I stand up and head for the shower.

CHAPTER 2

RIO

It's been a month since the bomb ripped through our world. And I've had patience. Too much. But all that changes tonight.

The old wooden floor creaks under my shoes as I stalk through Valentino's house. I came here to knock sense into him, to drag him out of his own stubborn skull. If he'd just left this house when he was supposed to, I wouldn't have had to go to the Puccinis for a favor.

And now that favor has cost me a lot. His men strut through the Boarpit like they own it, like we're theirs. Well, it ends tonight. Luciano can take this rotten, stubborn house and make of it whatever the fuck he wants. And I will do the same with his men.

"Valentino!" I roar, my voice cracking the silence. One last chance to get through his thick skull. One last chance before I make the choice for him.

Valentino is a virus, dull and steady, worming into systems and spreading until nothing works the way it should. Although to Brox and I, he's more of a hyena, one that will rip your throat if you step too close.

He has lived in Miami for over fifty years, but his Sicilian heritage, mafia roots, remain unmistakable. He is solely responsible for us being the mafia kingpins that we are today, ambitious, untested, and already carving our names into the city's underworld. He and his wife were our foster parents, but when his wife passed, he committed to raising us the 'right way.' He had been our Guardian and Warden, both our tormentor and protector, throughout much of our childhood. That lasted until the day we stood up to him. When I turned eighteen and we got a taste of money and power – small inheritance money came through, something our parents left for us. From that moment, he understood that if he ever crossed us again, we wouldn't hesitate to end him.

In a twisted way, we were lucky. Valentino took us under his wing and showed us the ropes. He fostered our devious way of thinking, and backed every bizarre idea we came up with, no matter how diabolical it was.

It was common knowledge that if we set a shed on fire, roughed up some older kids, or seriously harmed someone, Valentino would handle the situation, ensuring there were no repercussions for us.

I hear him downstairs, in the basement, and just as I'm about to head down, an unfamiliar sharpness in the air grabs me. A hint of something floral and spicy coming from the end of the hallway. It doesn't belong here. Not in this house.

I follow the scent as my steps quicken. I pass the staircase quietly and now I distinctly hear someone inside the bathroom.

I grab the cool brass doorknob and forcefully push the door open.

Steam from the shower fills the room, and there, standing in front of me, is a woman, her large breasts bouncing just like her tangled blond hair, which cascades down to the tops of her shoulders.

There are a few bruises blooming across her collarbone, her ribs, and one on her cheek. She reaches for a towel and wraps it quickly around her body.

Her bare feet are adorned with two metal shackles that bite into her ankles, a chain connects them and drags against the floor with every slight movement.

Before I even catch a glimpse of her face, a surge of anger overtakes me.

It's the same story, every damn time.

He finds them in the pits of the underworld, drug addicts or prostitutes, abuses them, disfigures them with his butchering skills, and finally, kills them. And then we have to take care of his mess. For something so stupidly insignificant, we could be made.

I grab her upper arm just as she finally lifts her head. What I see I'm not ready for; her eyes, almond-shaped and softly angled, green, remind me of a cat. But wilder. They're predator-like with thick lashes around them. Big bottom lip, little bow tie top. It almost knocks me out. Something happens to me right there and then, something ugly and... fuck knows, which riles me even more. I'm practically a God in my world, untouchable. Nobody can come within five feet of me without having their whole life flash in front of their eyes, and this woman... This woman provokes me in a way I've never been provoked.

"Who the fuck are you?" My voice is lethal.

She's stunned, like a rabbit caught in the headlights. Clearly, she doesn't know who I am. Otherwise she'd be cowering. They all do. "Don't make me repeat myself," I growl.

"L-Lana." she whispers.

"Get out." I say, as I grip on her arm firmly. Her eyes move on to someone behind me, and they become raw with fear, like the way someone stares at an oncoming train.

I turn to see Valentino standing in the doorway.

"Lana, this is my son, Rio. Rio, meet Lana." Valentino's voice is a calm command. "She's a guest in my house today. Isn't that right, Lana?"

He has another thing coming if he thinks I'm going to clean up his mess again.

I let go of Lana's arm and keep my eyes on Valentino. "What the fuck you think you're doing?" I growl.

"Manners, Rio," Valentino warns as Lana's gaze flickers between us.

"Go and get ready, honey." Valentino places his hand on the small of her back and guides her toward the basement door. "We haven't started playing yet."

Lana is reluctant to go back down the stairs, she must have figured that's a certain death for her, but Valentino shoves her.

"Lana. Get dressed and come back upstairs." I order her. Her shoulders ease, but just a fraction, as she looks down at her shackles.

"Valentino," I say. He knows what I mean. And he also knows deliberating for a second or a minute won't make a difference for me. I'll wait. With a creepy smile, he kneels down and unlocks the bolt holding the chain and the shackles. Then he strokes Lana's legs as he gets up.

"Go." I tell her, and I gesture to Valentino towards the living room. He turns on his heels, and I trail him. I'm fucking fed up with his antics.

He removes the apron he's wearing, stiff with dried blood, and drops it aside before sitting at the edge of the sofa.

"She's been given to me as a present, Rio." I hear his soft, but spine-tingling voice he always uses just before the monster inside him comes out. "Lana's been very naughty, and she needs to be punished. I was told to take my time."

It's the same unsettling and haunting voice that took us years to get over. Without him, we might never have become two of the most dreaded figures in Miami's underworld.

"You're out of your fucking mind if you think you're doing this." I growl. "We were clear. No more!"

He waves me off with a flick of his hand. He's waiting for Lana to show up at the doorway.

"Who gave her to you?" I ask.

"Virgil. You know him, he's one of Puccini's men."

I don't remember saving any of Valentino's victims. I never had a reason to. They were stupid enough to be lured by a predatory viper like him. This one deserves that ending too. No matter what she looks like and how she might taste. Fuck! I could ask him to let me fuck her before he has his way with her. Focus, asshole!

Valentino leans back and fixes his eyes on mine. Black as shoe polish, he sees my dark side better than I do. "You and Brox, you run this empire by the book. My way's like a tradition. You must dive deep into the blood of your enemies to truly appreciate their sacrifice. Keeps us strong. You could join me this time." He winks.

"You're a psychopath, Valentino!" I spit the word.

Lana's rigid silhouette appears in the doorway just as Valentino's sneer twists into something colder. His eyes narrow, hating the fact that he could never break me.

"Lana, I'll be in the basement. Preparing for you." He stands up and heads to the door. I know him; he'll be counting on me to step back. I have done that before.

"If I were you, I'd focus on packing." I stop him as he leaves. "We're not playing with the Puccinis anymore. You're on your own."

CHAPTER 3

LANA

I couldn't breathe, and I couldn't look away. Right in front of my eyes, nails were being pulled out, skin peeled, teeth taken out. The screams, oh God, they're burned into me. I'll never un-hear them.

But I didn't know that was a better nightmare than the one I'm in right now.

My sobbing was the mistake I made, one I will never make in my life again if I want to stay alive. They found me, Virgil and his buddy, and dragged me into this hellhole, but not before breaking me down with their fists. Serves me right for messing with their stuff.

Being here is surreal.

Valentino's initial demeanor was unsettlingly pleasant at first. But then I saw him for what he really was when he savagely dragged me down into the basement. It's when I saw them, those grotesque metal devices, covered in dried, congealed blood, like something out of a nightmarish documentary. The horrifying implication was crystal clear.

I screamed and pleaded, making desperate attempts to escape, but Valentino's eerie, unnerving calmness terrified me even more. Each time I struggled, he tightened the shackles, leaving me with a feeling of utter helplessness. Lucky for me he needed me clean for whatever he was going to do to me.

And now, I'm uncertain if I should feel fortunate or more terrified that his son, Rio, has appeared. He ordered me to get dressed, while Valentino remained silent, which means... something, I think.

He did what Rio told him to, and that counts.

My heart is pounding against my chest as I race down to the basement, frantically tearing through the rubbish. I spot my clothes, they're crumpled, filthy, but I don't care. I yank my black top over my head, drag my panties into place, and shove my legs into my jeans. My fingers fumble on the laces of my white sneakers, tying them in a blur. The moment they're tight enough, I sprint for the stairs, every muscle screaming for me to get out of this dungeon.

Hearing them in one of the rooms, I enter, my eyes moving between Valentino and Rio.

Rio's eyes lock onto mine for a fleeting moment before sliding down to scrutinize my top and jeans.

It's the first real chance I get to take him in. Dark hair, slicked back with effortless precision, every strand daring me to look closer. His eyes, intense, unyielding, catch mine, pinning me in place with a heat that makes my pulse falter. The tailored cut of his three-piece suit clings to him, radiating authority, every line sharpened to perfection. But it's the ink crawling up his neck, slipping out from beneath his collar, that betrays the truth, he's anything but reassuring.

"Lana," Valentino says as he moves past me, the unsettling proximity makes my stomach turn.

"I'll be waiting for you in the basement." Then he's gone, leaving me alone with Rio.

His words make me queasy, and my knees go weak. There's no doubt about it, he intends to complete what he began.

"Sit," Rio interrupts my train of thought.

I shake my head, refusing instinctively.

He exhales through his nose, already irritated with me. Without a word, he digs his cell from his pocket and dials.

"Virgil. It's Rio Boar." Rio's eyes narrow slightly as they track over my face, his jaw tight.

I hear the name, and a spike of terror shoots through me. My heart hammers so hard it feels like it might split my ribs. "No... no, you can't send me back to him." My voice breaks down, trembling on the edge of a sob. "Please."

Rio pauses, covering the mouthpiece with his palm. His unreadable gaze locks on mine.

I shake my head so hard, my vision blurs, and panic chokes me. "I'll do anything. Literally, anything. Please... don't send me back there."

"Hello? Rio, are you there?" I hear Virgil's voice, vile and slick, like rot given sound.

"Please! And don't leave me in here, too."
I'm desperate. "Whatever you say, I'll do."

He studies me for a beat.

His thumb hovers over the cell's screen, and
for a terrifying moment, I can't tell if he's about to
save me or hand me right back to the devil I ran
from. Then he sneers, his mouth twisting in a way
that freezes me in place.

"I'll call you back." He cuts the line.

Before he says anything to me, the low
rumble of a motorbike rolls through the silence.
The sound cuts off, replaced by the slam of the front
door and heavy footsteps pounding down the
hallway.

A tall, broad figure fills the doorway, head to
toe in a black padded leather jumpsuit. Helmet still
on. His attention shifts to me, and the helmet tilts.

Dramatically, he drags that dark, glossy
visor down the length of me. From my sneakers...
up my jeans... pausing just long enough at the curve
of my hips to make my skin prickle, then lingering
on my breasts a beat too long.

His head cocks slightly, like he's weighing
up a choice on a menu.

"Hey, brother," he says to Rio, and then his visor turns back to me.

With his helmet still on, the biker unbuttons his leather jacket, peeling it off in one smooth motion. It hangs low around his hips as he drops onto the couch beside Rio.

His black T-shirt clings on him like a second skin, stretched over ridged abs and broad pecs. The ink running up both arms speaks of fights that didn't just end in victory, but in finality.

That's the body of a man who never lost. Who never let someone walk away. And one look at him tells me if he wants to finish me, he will.

He reaches up, fingers gripping either side of the helmet, and lifts it off in one clean, practiced motion. The thing hits the coffee table with a dull thud.

Dark, wavy hair tumbles forward, a little messy, like he's just run his hands through it. A clean-shaven jaw, perfect brows, and pale blue eyes they almost glow.

He watches me closely, his gaze unhurried, and then his lips curl into a smile as he leans back into the sofa.

"I'm Brox." His chuckle is deep, edged with something that makes my stomach flip. "And you are?"

"L-Lana," My voice is unsteady, still broken with fear.

"You know you look like a fuckable sin, Lana?" Brox chuckles.

"Well," Rio says dryly, "this fuckable sin has just been handed over by Virgil to Valentino as a gift."

Brox's easy smile vanishes.

"Because, you know, he leaves no evidence." Rio concludes.

Brox's eyebrows draw together, and his gaze on Rio turns razor sharp. "Again? That's it! I'm gonna slit his fucking throat now."

"Yeah, let's do that," Rio replies, already pushing to his feet.

They move together like a storm front, big, intimidating, a wall of muscle and fury. I almost cheer them on.

From the hallway comes the thunder of boots on wood, they're pounding on a door so hard the frame shakes.

"He's locked himself in the basement," Rio growls. "No way to get to him right now."

"Valentino!" Brox roars, voice echoing off the walls. "You coward! Come out if you're a man!"

"Come on, let's not waste time. We got to get to the club," Rio says after a while of hammering. "I already told him to start packing, we won't be entertaining the Puccinis any longer."

While they're distracted in conversation, I shift, inch by inch, my heart pounding so loud I'm sure they'll hear it. My feet drag in tiny, shaky steps, each one a gamble as I slide down the hall. *God, please don't let them notice.* The hall stretches forever, and yet somehow, I reach it, the front door is only breaths away.

But out of nowhere, I'm yanked off balance, Rio's fingers fist in my hair and drag me up onto my toes. A sharp sting burns across my scalp as he jerks me forward and back, pulling my face next to his.

But out of nowhere, I'm yanked off balance, Rio's fingers fist in my hair and drag me up onto my toes. Pain sears my scalp as he jerks me forward, my face slammed close to his.

"Where're you going, princess?" his voice drips with mockery. "Or did you already forget what you said?"

I claw at his hand to ease the pull, twisting against his grip. "Let–me–go."

Brox strides into view, helmet in one hand, his gaze dragging over me from head to toe. He opens the front door and makes space for Rio and me to exit.

I'm dragged outside into the humid Miami air, with Brox following us, and already pulling on his padded biker suit.

"We're still missing quite a few pets," Brox swings a leg over his bike, looking at me.

"I was thinking the same thing."

"Let's try her out in the bar. Diego can handle her tonight. I know you're busy." His pale blue eyes engulf me like a waterfall. "Well, Lana, I'll see you later."

"Where are you taking me?" my voice wavers, but I try to fight back. "If you're going to kill me, do it now."

Rio releases my hair and laughs. Brox joins in.

"Kill you?" Brox slides his helmet on, visor snapping shut. "Oh, Lana…"

"We'll do everything but kill you," Rio finishes.

The roar of Brox's motorbike swallows the rest as he tears off down the street, leaving me with Rio, who clamps a hand around my upper arm and drags me toward a gleaming red Corvette.

BROX

The roar of my engine is the only thing loud enough to drown out my thoughts, but not for long. My grip on the handles tightens as I swerve past a line of palm trees, my bike growling beneath me like it knows I'm about to do something. The speedometer creeps up, 50… 60… 75. I let it. I'm not thinking. I don't want to think.

Still, her face won't get the fuck out of my head.

That mouth. That little chin tilt. Those eyes. Sin.

I know very well when my cock twitches, it usually means good times are coming.

I gun the throttle again and realize the road curves hard, I ease the brake just in time. My body leans with the bike, smooth, practiced, but my mind's still a fucking hurricane.

Why would Virgil want her dead? Do I want to know that? Or does it work well with our agenda? With the bomb explosion, our pets ran away. So far we've only got three back. Lucky for us, they came back willingly because they know we look after them.

I twist the throttle again and launch down a long, empty stretch of road.

I can't wait to see her sweat. She'll love it.

The Grand Bay Tower of Key Biscayne is getting closer. I take a hard turn, my tires squealing against the pavement as the streets narrow and the buildings get denser. I can feel the club looming now. The Boarpit is in the basement, with fifteen floors between it and our penthouse. Our kingdom.

I ride the bike into the underground garage, pressing the side button and waiting for the automatic gate to lift. The heat slams into me, all stale air and fumes. I ride it further in, park, kill the engine, and yank off my helmet.

CHAPTER 4

LANA

I stare at the road ahead, my pulse hammering. At least they didn't use me as a punching bag, like Virgil did, before putting me in a car.

"Where are you taking me?"

"To the Boarpit," Rio says flatly, his eyes never leaving the road.

The name means nothing to me, but the way he says it makes my stomach knot. "And what exactly happens there?"

He glances at me, just once. "That depends."

"On what?" My voice is sharper than I intended. "If I'm going to die there, I'd rather you tell me now."

His hands stay steady on the wheel. "If I were going to kill you, you'd already be dead. I thought we'd already established that."

I don't answer, I just fold my arms tight across my chest.

"Who do you live with?" his voice sounds almost human now.

My throat dries. "No one."

"What about your family? Where are your parents?"

My parents? Died the same year I turned eighteen. Cancer. Everyone said I was lucky to dodge foster care but fuck that luck when you're alone. I had plans, I went to med school for a year before I had to give it all up. Before my life turned upside down.

"Dead."

"Friends? Roommates? Someone who's going to come looking for you?"

"No one," I say.

Mateo. He was the only one there for me. Feeding me when I couldn't afford any food, sharing his bed with me because he knew I didn't have anyone, and anywhere to stay.

But Mateo is dead now. And I'm trying so hard to forget his death. The more I try, the harder it hits me. His screams are still etched into my skull.

"How do you know Virgil?" he continues with his questions.

"I don't know him."

"Okay." He shifts his tone. "Why would he leave you at Valentino's?"

"Why would you have a killer for a father?" I dare to ask.

From the corner of my eye, I catch him glancing at me.

"He was my foster parent. Now answer my question. Why does Virgil want you dead?"

I keep my gaze locked on the road and lift my shoulders in a small shrug. The only answer he'll get.

Seeing that I won't say a word, he exhales in frustration.

We drive the rest of the way in silence, with my mind replaying his questions. I might have told him I'm totally disposable. Then again, he probably knew that the second he saw me at Valentino's.

By the time we cross the bridge into Key Biscayne, the streets grow quieter. The Corvette rolls onto a side street lined with palms, stopping in front of a tall tower with blacked-out windows.

At its base, a steel door glows under low light. Above it, in sharp cursive script, The Boarpit. On the side, a 3D emblem of two boars locked in a brutal clash.

The moment the car stops, two men in black suits step forward. One opens my door, but before I can step out, Rio has gone around and is waiting for me there. His palm presses against the small of my back, firm enough to steer me exactly where he wants me to go.

We step inside, and I realize the Boarpit is a club. Inside the air is thick, heavy with the scent of sweat and alcohol. Music pounds from below, a relentless bass that rattles my ribcage, and makes the floor vibrate beneath my feet.

I hesitate, just for a breath.

"You'll start at the bar," he says without looking at me.

At the bar? I'll be working at the bar?

Just before we reach a set of steel stairs, Rio stops. He leans in and talks in my ear.

"We have people at every exit and entrance. Behave, and you'll live." His eyes meet mine, and for a second, I think he's about to soften, until his next words slice that thought apart. "Run, and I'll slit your throat before you reach the door."

I bob my head in a shaky nod, the only thing I can manage.

Out of nowhere, Brox materializes in front of us, his massive frame blocking out the strobing lights. He's changed into a striking three-piece suit that makes him untouchable, just like Rio's.

"They need you." Brox nods toward somewhere in the club, and Rio walks off without a word.

"Lana." My stomach knots hearing my name. "Follow me."

I trail after him through the crowd, weaving between strangers who smell like alcohol and sweat, the floor sticky under my shoes.

Brox stops at the bar. "Diego, this is Lana."

Diego's voice is nearly swallowed by the crowd, but I catch the low roll of an accent over my name. He's older, maybe in his forties, with a rough, dangerous edge.

"Nice to meet you," My voice is barely steady.

He smirks, pours himself a shot, and downs it without looking away. "Good luck."

The words feel less like encouragement and more like a warning.

Brox crooks a finger at a blonde across the room. She moves toward us instantly, like she's been trained to respond. They exchange a few words too quiet for me to catch, then Brox turns and walks away without looking back.

The blonde, who introduces herself as Jo, orders me. "Go change and find me." She points to the door behind the bar. "Oh, and make sure you talk to Dr. Morales."

Diego points to the entrance of the bar, from where I can get to the changing room. Who's Dr. Morales? Inside, a rack of identical black mini dresses hangs against the wall next to the door, every one cut to show too much skin, the same dress as Jo is wearing. There's nothing else, no other option. My throat tightens. I grab one and slip it on, hating how it looks on me. It's a low-plunge halter neck with a flippy hem mini skater dress.

Black stilettos litter the floor, and I find my size, a pair that fits me perfectly. I slide them on, feeling the arch bite into my feet already.

For a moment, I freeze at the mirror. I was never one of those pretty girls, the kind who dress like their flesh is up for sale. So it feels like a stranger staring back. I yank my hair into a low, slick ponytail, tight enough to sting, and in the small chaos of makeup I see, I find foundation and apply it on my face, over my bruise.

"You look good in that dress." I scream and stumble back, my heart jumping into my throat. An elderly woman appears out of nowhere, her dark hair tied in a low bun. The changing room is not small, but I should have seen her. Maybe because everything in here is black, and she's wearing black too, like I am, now.

"I'm sorry, I didn't mean to scare you." She's holding a pen and a notebook in her hands. "I'm Dr. Morales. What's your name, dear?"

"Um, Lana."

She notes it down. "Lana what?"

"Lana Rayne." I say.

"Married?" she keeps noting down my answers.

"No."

"Boyfriend?"

"Um, no." What's with the questions?

"When was the last time you had sex, Lana?" she looks at me, waiting to judge me whatever I say.

"With all due respect, that's none of your business, Dr. Morales."

"So, it's been a few years then," she concludes and notes it down. I don't correct her. It's been over three years.

"You can go now. Have a good time, dear."

"T-thank you?" My forehead creases in confusion.

When I step back out, Diego's eyes sweep over me, slow and deliberate. I forgot I had changed into this dress. His brow lifts, lips forming a silent "O." I don't need to hear the wolf whistle to know it's there.

Jo's waiting, already impatient. She rattles off instructions, how to serve drinks, where to go, the details are common sense, but the way she speaks makes it clear, it's not advice, it's orders.

Rio saved me from certain death, and he's taken me here to pay back the favor by serving drinks? I will do the best I can.

I start serving, I've done this before. I weave through bodies, balancing trays of drinks, the music pounding so loud it swallows my every thought. No one's watching to see if I'm doing a good job, and that's fine with me.

Soon, I find the club swallows me whole. Heat presses in from every direction, the scent of alcohol and bodies almost suffocating. Strobing lights catch glimpses of faces, laughing, shouting, leering. I move through it all like a ghost.

Behind the bar, Diego's hands move fast, sliding drinks my way, nodding toward tables. No small talk. No softness. Just the constant churn of orders and the bass pounding in my chest like a second heartbeat, a reminder I'm alive, for now.

After three, maybe four hours, the ache in my feet is a dull throb with every step, and my throat is scraped raw from shouting orders over the music.

"Take these to Luciano." Diego's voice yanks me out of my thoughts as he slides a tray of drinks into my hands.

"I'm sorry, who?" Surely, he doesn't expect me to know the regulars.

"Over there, through the black doors." He nods and repeats. "Luciano."

I only now see that the west wall of the club is a large doorway with the words Black Chamber etched in black metal on top of it, illuminated faintly from behind. The doors are made of black, heavy wood that seem to swallow the light around it. They're almost invisible. I hesitate for a fraction of a second too long, and he rolls his eyes. "Now, Lana."

I nod, gripping the tray with both hands as I make my way to the Black Chamber. I nudge the door with my hip, and it swings open almost at once. It's too dark inside, but even so, I recognize Brox's blue eyes, they shine in the dark.

He keeps the door open for me, but his eyes don't move from my body, trailing over me unashamedly, like a predator sizing up his prey. His eyes sharpen in sudden recognition. "Lana?"

He steps in closer, gaze sweeping me from head to toe. "Fuck me."

"Um, Diego asked me to deliver this to someone called Luciano."

He repeats slower, the words sounding like they've been ripped from somewhere dark inside him. "Fuck. Me."

"Um, yeah." His stare burns, and I can't bring myself to meet it.

He shuts the door behind me, his eyes running down the back of my dress now. Then his gaze swings back to me. "A walking sin!"

He nods toward the hall. "Luciano's five doors down."

I walk slowly with the tray of drinks through the dark corridor, watching my step. I notice the air-conditioning here works better, or at least the air is different, lighter, cooler. As I pass by the first door, I hear strange sounds coming from behind it. Moaning, groaning, squealing, everything really. Walking past door number two makes me realize the hubbub from the club has died down and now it feels like I stepped into another world. In here the walls are lined with black velvet, the carpet is black and only now do I notice each door having a gilded number on them, and a golden door handle.

Door number three is open and I'm curious, and peek inside. A full-figured naked woman lies on her back on a lounge chair, and a man standing in front of her is holding her legs, and fucking her, with three others waiting for their turn behind him. Another man stands over her face, ejaculating ropes of semen over her open mouth. A fourth man comes into motion, tries to sit on her face, and gets her to suck his balls. And succeeds.

One of the men catches my eye and pumps his cock in my direction.

I flinch, the drinks wobbling on my tray and I hurry off, scanning the corridor for door five, to find Luciano.

I spot door five half-open and pause to knock. I know I could peek inside, but I choose not to.

"Drinks for Luciano." I say.

"Gentleman, our drinks are here." Thunderous laughter ripples from inside before the door swings wide. Standing before me is Luciano, I presume, completely naked. He's probably in his sixties, with a large stomach that strangely doesn't affect his confidence because behind him, there are three or four younger men, half naked. In the background I see a woman on the floor, sitting upside down, with body twisted like a prawn, her cunt and ass up in the air. She's leaned on the lounge chair and that way, it allows men to stand over her, and alternate fucking her ass and cunt as they do.

"Come inside, please." He ushers me in.

I'd rather not, but the air in here is different somehow. The light breeze in my face from the air conditioning is almost welcoming. With each step I take inside, the increasing oxygen becomes apparent. I try to leave the drinks on the closest table without any curiosity on my part, but for some reason, I want to look further inside the room.

As I observe, my pulse quickens, each beat echoing in my ears until it drowns out the room. A slow heat spreads through me, curling low in my stomach. When Luciano's hand slides onto my lower back, it's like my body is no longer mine. The touch sinks deep, electric and heavy all at once, pulling me into a haze where thought is slow and sensation is everything. I'm tuned only to that point of contact, caught in it, almost craving it, even though some buried part of me knows I shouldn't.

Another woman is held upright between two men, being spit-roasted, while she moans loudly, enjoying herself.

Suddenly there is an ache under my skin that I can't disguise. Luciano answers without hesitation, his hand stroking me in one unbroken glide, up my back, curving under my arm, slipping beneath the fabric of my dress like it belongs there. Rough fingers claim my breast, pinching my already stiffened nipple, and the shock of it sends a shiver straight through my spine. My knees threaten to give, but his grip holds me in place, forcing me to feel every deliberate second of it.

It's strange, infuriating, even, because I don't find him attractive, and yet the way he touches me is maddening, winding heat through my veins like smoke I can't escape.

The bliss is ripped away in an instant. Another hand clamps around my arm like a steel trap, tearing me from the old man's grasp. My breath catches in shock, and I look up, straight into Rio's towering frame, his eyes burning with a mix of fury and something far more dangerous.

"Who the fuck let you in here?" he snarls, his voice low, lethal. "Get. Out."

He yanks me away without a word, dragging me down the long hallway like I weigh nothing. My heels scrape against the floor, my breath ragged, until he shoves me through the double doors with a force that sends me stumbling, crashing to my knees on the sticky floor.

I stay there, palms flat against the grime, my heart pounding so hard it hurts. My cheeks burn with a toxic mix of humiliation and rage.

I scramble to my feet before the crowd can trample me, forcing my legs to carry me back to my station, back to the job I was doing before it all went sideways.

The rush still lingers, stubborn and unwanted, coiling low in my stomach. But it's fading fast, leaving me cold and furious at myself for even feeling it. My skin burns where I was touched, and I hate it.

I move through the rest of my shift in a daze, the haze of the Black Chamber clinging to me like perfume I can't wash off. Every time my mind slips, I'm back there. The rest of the night blurs; I'm taking orders, delivering drinks, smiling when I have to, but it's all mechanical.

The club slowly empties, the bass fading to a low, pulsing hum that echoes in my bones. One by one, the staff filter out, leaving me with the shadows and the memory of something I can't shake.

"Lana, here's a five-hundred-dollar tip from Luciano." Diego counts the money on the counter. I'm shocked, glancing around to see if this is some kind of joke. But the only person nearby is Jo, cleaning the tables and ignoring us completely. Five hundred dollars for groping?

"For me?"

"Yeah, he's a great tipper. But I'll let Rio give you the money." He chuckles and scoops the cash, dropping it into the till. "See you tomorrow." Diego grabs his bag from the bar chair and heads out.

"You did good tonight, Lana. Go change, and I'll see you later." Jo waves casually and walks away.

"Thank you." I head to the changing room to slip back into my clothes. My skinny jeans and my top are much more comfortable than the black dress and the stilettos. I smile to myself. I can't believe this is it.

When I come out, the place is empty. Everyone's gone. I can leave if I want to because no one's at the door.

"Rio Boar!"

The voice booms through the space. I know it instantly. I drop behind the bar, clutching the counter as if it could save me, my heart hammering so violently I can taste blood in my throat. It's Virgil.

Did Rio call him? Did he bring me here just to hand me over? Of course he did. He used me tonight, and I'm not needed any longer.

From where I'm crouching, I see the black double doors slightly ajar. I must hide. Quietly, keeping myself hidden, I slip inside.

CHAPTER 5

BROX

The aftertaste of bad tequila and sex hangs in the air, thick and stale, even with the club's doors shut.

I push through the curtain at the back, into the narrow steel stairwell that leads up to my office. That's where the real stuff is, surveillance, books, and keeping eyes on the Black Chamber rooms we never advertise. Tonight, I'm also the one closing up.

The office sits high above the main floor, tucked at the back like a watchtower. One entire wall is a dark-glass window, pitch-black from the outside, a perfect mirror of the chaos below. But from inside, I can see everything. Every face. Every deal. Every mistake.

I drop into the chair, put my shoes up on the desk, and watch the empty club for a moment. Peaceful, in its own way.

Then I see the folder with Lana's name on it. Sol's contact at the force gets us anything we need.

Lana Rayne. Twenty-one years old. Parents deceased. No next of kin.

I flip the page. She's not married. No boyfriends. No sex for at least two years. Perfect. Dr. Morales did a good job, too.

Then I turn toward the east wall, floor-to-ceiling monitors, black-and-white feeds flickering. Most nights, I scan for trouble. Not tonight. Tonight, my eyes go straight to room five.

Luciano's room. The one I sent Lana into.

I was waiting to see what would happen, but Rio sent me to deal with the security issue. From the look on his face when I returned, something had happened. I hit play. No skips. No jumps. I want to see every second.

I see her reaching Luciano's room and being ushered by him as she's carrying the drinks. By the time she lowers the tray on the side table, the air has already hit her. Luciano, the asshole, knows very well.

He touches her back. Strokes her. When his hand slips under her dress, my teeth grit. I thought it'd be fun to watch, but for some reason, it's not. I don't want anyone touching her before I do.

He pinches her breast, and her eyes flutter shut, she's starting to enjoy it. She doesn't know there's something in the air in that room. We designed it that way. We want them warm. We want them pliable.

I'm glad Rio came when he did, even if the way he yanked her out was rough.

I rewind. Watch it three more times. Each time, my fists clench tighter when I see Luciano touching her. Then I freeze the frame on Lana, lips parted, eyes half-closed.

I'm angry, and horny at the same time. I scrub through the rest of the feed, checking to see where she is right now. After a few minutes of searching, I finally found her crouching under the bar. She thinks she'll hide in there? Cute.

But then I see Virgil at the entrance, Sol and Rio next to him, talking, and I realize who she's hiding from. I go back to Lana, and see her moving clandestinely in the dark, slipping back inside the Black Chamber, and straight into room two. Silly girl.

The lighting's dim, but I can see her pacing. She runs her hands through her hair, then over her arms. She's restless, electric.

This will be fun.

The room's ventilation is tweaked in here too, more oxygen and a touch of maca root. Rio calls it "social lubricant." I call it "competitive advantage." A special concoction that doesn't touch the men, only the women.

I can tell the second it hits her. She slows, sinks into the mattress, lets her head fall back. Her breathing deepens; lips part just a little. She shivers and then smiles at nothing.

I could watch this forever.

She stretches out, arms overhead, the top riding up just enough to show skin. Not for anyone else, just for herself. She closes her eyes, fingers tracing lazy circles over her ribs, her hips, her stomach.

I tilt the camera, zoom in a little. She's beautiful, even in grainy black and white.

I pull my whisky bottle from the drawer with a glass and pour myself a finger.

"Cheers, sunshine," I whisper, and watch her try to outrun herself.

I put my hands behind my head. This is better than TV.

She keeps her sneakers on for the first five minutes, then she sits up, kicks off one sneaker, then the other. She glances at the door, listening to footsteps, but the hallway outside is empty. There's no one left to see her except me, and I'm not about to look away.

She lies back, arms stretched overhead, the thin tank top clinging to her chest. The cotton rides up, exposing a strip of stomach, a flash of hip. Her breathing is shallow, uneven, like she's halfway between panic and relief. She presses her palms over her eyes, rubs hard.

She turns onto her side, pulls the comforter up, then lets it drop. Her thighs scissor, restless. Her fingers trace the seam of her jeans, then drift up to the hem of her shirt. She hesitates, then slips her hand underneath, fingertips skating over her breast. She palms it, slow, cautious, thumb circling until her nipple stiffens and pushes the fabric out.

Her teeth bite down on her lower lip. Her hips arch, just a little.

Fuck me.

My own breath catches, embarrassingly loud in the dead air of my office. I palm my cock over my pants, but I don't stroke myself, not yet. I want to watch her longer.

She rubs her thighs together, legs straight and toes pointed, like she's anchoring herself to the mattress. Then she moves her hand lower, down her stomach, pausing at the waistband of her jeans. She unbuttons them, and slips her fingers inside, just the tips at first. She closes her eyes, lips parted, breathing in little bursts I can count on the camera.

She starts slowly, hips rolling barely an inch, just enough to grind against her own hand. Her other arm drapes over her face, blocking the light. I zoom in, losing the edges of the frame, focusing just on the little triangle of movement where her hand disappears under denim.

I can't help myself. I shift in my chair, adjust the bulge in my pants. I want to be in that room, to see the color in her cheeks, the heat radiating off her skin. But even on the screen, it's perfect.

She works herself with patience, never rushing, just building and building. Her mouth twists, eyebrows drawn together, fighting to keep quiet. She turns her face into the pillow, probably muffling a whimper. She speeds up, hips jerking sharper, knees starting to tremble.

I wonder who she's imagining. I want it to be me. I want her to know I'm watching.

She gasps, chokes down a moan, and goes rigid. For a second, she's stone-still, every muscle tensed. Then she shudders, her whole body arching off the bed before collapsing. Her hand stays buried for a long time, fingers flexing in slow, lazy pulses, squeezing every last drop of pleasure out of herself.

She lies there, sweaty, and half undressed, and finally lets her breath out in a long, shaky exhale.

I don't even realize I'm palming myself until the whiskey bottle tips over, spilling across my lap. I curse, grab a handful of napkins, mop up the mess. I'm hard as steel, and for a second, I think about just finishing it right here.

But I don't.

I watch her pull her hand out, wipe it on the sheet, and smile at herself. She buttons her jeans, sits up, runs fingers through her hair.

I'm not waiting any longer. I head for the stairwell. I don't care if anyone sees my hard-on. Lana Rayne, you just made my night.

My zipper's still straining from the show Lana just put on and I know I could take a second to fix it, get my shit together, but fuck that. The only thing worse than being a horny idiot is pretending you're not.

I make it to the main floor, the now empty club.

"Jesus' fuck, get a grip," I mutter to myself but my hands do the opposite, adjusting my crotch like it'll make the hard-on disappear.

I snake through the side hallway and stop outside room two. For a second, I think about turning around and letting her sleep.

But that's not what I do. That's not who I am.

I open the door just wide enough to slide through, then close it behind me. She lifts her head, those wild green eyes locking onto mine like they're holding me in place.

"Hello Lana. What are you doing in here?"

"Brox!" she startles when she sees me and swiftly ensures her decency by smoothing her jeans and top. "I-I'm sorr–"

"Do you know we don't keep our pets on this floor?" I walk up to her, using all my strength to stop myself from bending her down and fucking her into oblivion.

"Um, I-I don't know what you mean," she can't focus, it's starting again, the orgasm she had ripples through her body and she needs another one. And I can give it to her.

"You're our pet," I take her chin in my hand, slow enough that she could break away if she wanted. She wouldn't, I know. I angle her face up, study the stubborn line of her jaw, the lustful wilderness in her eyes. She's ready for a kiss. But I won't give it to her, yet.

"And in this room, we play with our pets." My thumb brushes her cheek and immediately, she closes her eyes, tuning into my touch. Fuck, I'll come in my pants seeing her so raw.

I let go of her chin, step back just enough to force her to follow if she wants more. I watch her weigh the options, see the calculation in her eyes.

"Let me show you."

I lie on the bed and pat the space in front of me.

"Take off your clothes for me, Lana."

There is no thought process at all. Her clothes come off in an instant. Jeans, top, panties. Presenting me with the body of a goddess. There are some bruises on it, although I'm not worried, soon they'll be gone. Her breasts are ample, like God was making them for my hands.

She lies down facing me, but I turn her around and press her back to my front. She may not like it, but I prefer this position, because that'll keep her open for more.

She turns her head, tries to kiss me as I hold her down, my hands roaming over her breasts, stroking, kneading and pinching her beautiful hard nipples. I bite into her shoulder, gentle at first, harder after, and I listen to her beautiful moans. I know she wants that. She needs that. Any touch. For hours.

I'm close to bursting, I know I'm going to give in. I yank the button of my pants open, and drag the zipper down with no patience, freeing my stealthy cock. I realize the precum has been leaking in my pants, from torturing it for so long.

My arm slides beneath her neck, dragging her face toward mine. I crush my mouth against hers, and she kisses me like she's starving. My free hand pushes between her legs. She's soaked in her arousal, throbbing with need.

I can't wait any longer, I grab her inner thigh from below and lift her knee as I position myself at her entrance. Doing it without protection is a big no in our world, but this little gem appears to be clean, as per Dr. Morales advice.

I'm big, and girthy, I know that. Women often complain, quite a few have cried, but I pay no notice. I slide in her cunt like it's my home, her arousal letting me enter her fully. But it's the sudden whimper she does that throws me off. I pull out, I mustn't cum so stupidly soon, and then enter her again. We're lying sideways, I support her inner thigh as her leg is held up, and my other arm has her in chokehold, holding on her as leverage as I start to slam inside this little sweet cunt.

She moans, long, deep at first, with each of my stroke her body jerks, her fucking insane tits bounce, I'm close to coming but I won't, I'm going to make it last for her. I pull out and she's desperate immediately, searching for my cock with her hand like a starved whore. But I open her knee wider, and as sloppy my cock is with her arousal, I push it against her ass. She whimpers at first, but her desire, her thirst overpowers her, and as I edge slowly in, her moans get longer, from pain, I know, as she adjusts, but also because she needs me. Some women don't want to be fucked in their ass but then again, no one's asking. I certainly am not. I'm in fully, to the hilt now, and I slowly pull out, and start again.

Her cries hit harder than any drug I've ever tasted, she seems to be flying, engrossed in the fucking that she hasn't seen Rio standing next to us. He must have seen us on the CCTV.

He's pumping his cock right now, preparing for the space I've been making for him. He's finished putting on the condom, probably he hasn't read her file yet, and kneels on the bed. He holds her leg higher, as he positions himself at her entrance.

Her eyes open in a trance, and she smiles, showing her beautiful white teeth.

She is in so much need I'm not sure we'll be able to sate her, but fuck me she's horny and willing. And it's how I want my women.

The moment Rio is in, he fills the room with his groan. He pulls out, and that's when I go balls deep in her ass, her sweet moans add to the whole experience. We alternate, Rio's in to the hilt, and when he comes out, I enter her, that way she's constantly fucked. He's holding her leg, kneading her tits, then slapping them over and sideways as we're undulating together, working her needs. Women in these rooms need the touch, the slap, the pinch, we know what they crave and we give it to them. With my chokehold I hold her body in place, and my other hand is between her legs, pinching it as she screams in orgasm after orgasm.

"More, m-more, don't stop..." She breathes like a nymph and whines long, and soft.

"Who's our star pet tonight?" I slam into her ass, I'm really close to coming.

"I am.." she huffs. I am... I-I am.."

"Yes, you are, Lana. You're a big girl now." I say and keep ramming into her ass, as Rio thrusts deep in her cunt at the same time.

"Do you wanna be a big girl, Lana?" Rio slaps her cheek softly.

"I do.. I am." Her eyes are rolling back from the orgasms she's having.

I growl as I cum in her ass and still inside her body until every last drop is squeezed out of me, while Rio continues ramming into her fast, picking up speed, and annihilating her body, "Fuck, Brox I can go on forever with this little whore."

Then he quickly pulls out, removes the condom and goes on his knees to put his cock inside Lana's mouth as he's cumming. She has her tongue out already and is hungrily trying to suck and lick it as he's spurting rope after rope over her face, and mouth.

Rio growls loudly when he's done. He looks at her from above and chuckles. "Whores live of cum." He takes a drop of his cum off of her cheek, and then lets her suck it off his finger. "Yeees, you know it.."

She grins and nods. It's impossible tonight, but it's sure good to know how many cocks this little slut can take in one go. That's a task for tomorrow, I think.

CHAPTER 6

RIO

The elevator doors part with a quiet hiss, and the moment we step out, the air shifts.

Our penthouse is all glass and shadow, with Miami glittering beneath us like it's ours to burn.

I head straight for the mini bar, my shoes clicking against the polished marble. I need something in my hand that isn't a gun... or a mistake.

My reflection stares back from the black glass cabinet, my hair is still messed up from the fucking, my shirt open at the throat, my veins in my neck tight.

I pour whiskey to the line in the tumbler and swallow hard. Heat climbs my throat, spreading under my sternum. My jaw works like it's chewing through a problem that refuses to yield.

Behind me, Brox carries Lana.

She's tucked against his chest, one arm under her knees, the other braced at her back. Her hair is damp from all the fucking we did, she's naked, and I can't stop looking at her skin.

I don't know why it's different. I've been with enough women in my life to know better.

Brox moves like a soldier leaving a blast zone with the only thing worth saving. I don't say a word, if I do, it'll come out as something I can't take back.

"Bedroom," I grunt, anyway.

He's already heading there.

The penthouse is quiet at this time of night, with Greta not being here. I follow him down the hall until he steps into the guest room and lowers her to the bed the way a bomb tech sets down a live charge, careful, exact.

What the fuck is wrong with him? Or me, watching him like this?

He covers her with a silk sheet, smoothing it once at her shoulder. I lean on the doorway, the glass of whisky heavy in my hand, still not sure what to make of tonight. It was a blast, that's for sure. From the moment I saw her in Valentino's bathroom, I wanted to fuck her. Now that I have, I should be done.

Instead, I'm losing my mind.

Her eyelids flutter, a soft sigh slipping out. The club's air still clings to her, my blend, my poison, designed to nudge women past their own lines. I built those rooms. I know exactly what's in them.

I drain the glass and turn around, needing more. Brox follows me into the living room, and I pour him a glass, too.

"Here." I pass it over and drop onto the sofa, one half of me calm, the other angrier than I've ever been in my life.

"Don't look at me like that," Brox says, settling into the leather chair opposite. "I'm doing this for you. I can tell how much you like her."

The glass sweats in my palm. "You don't get to tell me what I like."

"You think I don't see it? The way you watch her?"

"Fuck you." I tip back the whiskey, slam the glass down. "I was going to kill Luciano Puccini tonight."

He doesn't flinch.

"But when I saw her in his room..." My teeth grind. "I had to change the plan. What the fuck were you thinking, sending her to him?"

"You're overreacting."

My laugh is short, ugly. "Overreacting? You handed her to that bastard on a silver plate."

His jaw flexes. Nothing else.

"You fucked everything up." My nostrils flare. "I had him. Two seconds from pulling the trigger."

"You know why you didn't do it?" Brox leans closer, his eyes fixed on mine. "Because you like her. That's why. It's why you told Virgil we don't have her."

My teeth clench so tight my jaw aches. "That's not how it was."

"Then say it." His eyes narrow, daring me. "Say you don't want her and I'll send her down, with the other girls. Where she belongs."

The silence between us is a noose. I could lie. I don't.

I stand, pacing to the window. On one side, the night stretches dark over the ocean. I've killed for every inch of this view, and yet all I can think about is the woman in my penthouse.

Lana Rayne.

Now wrapped in my sheets.

And I hate Brox for putting her there.

I hate myself more for wanting to go back in that room.

Brox breaks the quiet. "You think I don't know you, Rio? You've been off ever since Valentino's. You kill for fun. No one stops you."

"Watch yourself."

"I am." His voice drops, dangerous. "You're not."

We lock eyes. But right now, we're two predators circling the same prey. And I can't decide if I want to punch him... or thank him.

I go to the bar and pour myself another whiskey, but don't drink it. My mind's already back in that room, Lana's skin pale against the sheets, breathing soft, lips parted like she's dreaming.

We're so tightly wound into each other that the faintest sound, a soft, caught breath from the bedrooms, cuts clean through, breaking the air between us.

It's Lana. Wrapped in the sheet, hair tangled, eyes blinking against the low light.

Brox's head snaps toward her, his lips parting like he's forgotten how to breathe. I see him too.

She clutches the sheet to her chest, the fabric creased in her fists. Her gaze flicks between us in confusion.

"Where am I?" she asks.

"Our place," I say. "The penthouse."

Brox's cock is hard again, he fixes it in his pants, and if I'm honest, I could continue fucking her into the night, but I'm bracing for the questions that often come soon after they wake up. About what got to them in the Black Chamber. That's usually the deal breaker.

Her gaze roams all over, the furniture, mini bar, at the open kitchen in the distance. When her eyes find mine again, she still has that look on her, desirable, untamed, with a flicker of need she can't hide.

"Water," Brox says. He's already moving, snatching a bottle from the kitchen, pouring into a glass. He hands it to her like he's done it a thousand times, though I've never seen him do that for anyone. Then he sits in his chair.

She drinks deep, she must be parched. Hell, we all are. When she finishes, she passes the glass back to Brox before turning to me.

"W-what did Virgil want? Was he looking for me?"

"What do you think?" I ask, keeping my voice even.

She just gives me that same shrug I got in the car. "Did you tell him I work for you now?"

"Were you working for him before?" my gut tightens. Fuck.

She shakes her head. "No. Never."

"Then what happened that makes him want you dead so badly?"

"I-I saw him k-kill someone," her eyes glisten.

Brox's voice softens. "Oh, cupcake. Come here."

She folds into him, curling up on the chair as he wraps his arms around her.

"It was horrible," she says, her words muffled against his chest.

"What a shame," Brox murmurs, stroking her hair, and locks eyes with me. This is good. Really good. We've got something else on the Puccinis now, a witness who could put Virgil away if we wanted to.

"Um, can I ask you something?" she lifts her head at me. "Earlier I made five hundred bucks from that guy in the Black Chamber. When will I get my money?"

"Your money?" I ask, fixing her with a stare. I get she might be confused, but I want her to see what's really going on.

"Y-yeah."

"That money is mine, Lana, not yours. I pay for your upkeep, and you pay me back by servicing my clients in the Black Chamber."

This is the moment she should connect the dots about what she's doing here, and about the air in the rooms. It's the moment she should threaten to call the cops... or retreat and run the first chance she gets. There's no middle ground. So we know where she stands.

"Your job as our pet, is to work in the Black Chamber, sunshine." Brox reiterates.

I wait for the penny to drop. She saw what was happening there.

"So, I won't get the money, is that what you're saying?" she's either too focused on the money, or burying herself in distraction, pretending none of what I'm saying matters.

"Lana," I say, leaning forward. She's definitely not getting it. "Let me make this crystal clear for you, princess. You are free to go back to Valentino's and to Virgil's if you want. But you probably know what's going to happen to you if you do. Your other and only option is working for us, in the Black Chamber. You'll get no money. No freedom. Basically, you get nothing. But we'll feed you. And keep you happy. That's it. The choice is yours."

Her gaze flicks between us. "O-of course I don't want to go to Virgil, or Valentino's."

Has she really not processed what we're saying?

"So you're happy to stay? Is that it?" Brox asks.

She shrugs, then suddenly grows serious. "What if I need money for something? Like, tampons or razors, I dunno. Or panties. Clothes."

"We'll provide everything you need. And more." Brox winks at her, and she goes utterly still, her green eyes growing wider.

"Um, you should know what I did downstairs, I don't do that often." Her eyes shift between us. "I mean, at all. Not for a long time."

"Not for a long time?" my brow arches. Brox's mouth tilts in a half-smirk.

"No." She bites her lower lip. "I'm sorry. I don't know what got over me."

"Well, fuck me, Lana Rayne," Brox exclaims. "Because I want that to get over you again."

She smiles, blushing. "Did you happen to pick up my clothes? They're the only ones I have."

"We'll get you new ones. Go rest. It's almost three in the morning," I tell her.

CHAPTER 7

BROX

The first thing I register is the smell. Coffee. Strong, black, bitter enough to kick the sleep out of me. Greta's way of saying get your ass up without words.

I push a palm over my face and crack my eyes open. She's standing at the foot of my bed in her neat black uniform, hair scraped into that severe bun like she's about to take a mugshot. The cup and saucer in her hands look like they belong in some hotel suite, not in the apartment of two men who've buried more than one problem under concrete.

"Morning, Mr. Boar," she says, gliding forward.

"Jesus fuck, Greta, we've talked about this. Stop calling me that." My voice is rough, sleep still lodged in my throat.

Greta has been with us since day one. She knows us, what we want, how we want it, and delivers each time.

Her eyebrow flicks up, her version of a smirk, and she sets the cup on the nightstand. "You'll want it hot."

I swing my legs out of bed. "Rio up already?"

"He left for the gym before sunrise. Came back about twenty minutes ago."

Figures. My brother treats his workouts like religion. I pick up the coffee, take a long sip, and feel the heat cut through the fog in my head.

I don't drink it here. Instead, I walk barefoot across the marble floors, coffee in hand, and make my way out of the bedroom.

The kitchen's at the far end, pass the living space. It's all black marble and steel, sharp enough to cut yourself on if you're not careful. I take a seat at the island, set the coffee down, and let the morning sink in.

The quiet doesn't last.

"Morning," Rio says, his voice carrying from behind me.

I glance over my shoulder. He's fresh from the shower, hair damp, towel slung low on his hips. The tattoos crawling up his neck are still beaded with water. He's got that look, the one that says he's already been planning the day while most people were still drooling into their pillows.

"Morning," I reply, watching as he crosses to the fridge, grabs a bottle of water, and downs half of it in one go.

"I've got the meeting downstairs," he says, wiping his mouth with the back of his hand.

"With the four idiots who think their app's worth ten million?"

He smirks. "They're not idiots. Just desperate."

I lift my cup. "Don't take less than fifty-one percent. We need that one percent."

"Don't worry. I know what I'm doing." He takes another swig, then glances toward his bedroom. "I'll be in the boardroom by ten." He disappears down the hall toward his room.

I take another drink of coffee, letting the bitterness sit on my tongue. The boardroom. The heart of The Boarpit's real business. Next to the office, overlooking the club like a goddamn throne room. Deals get signed there. Alliances sealed. Sometimes bodies, too, the black marble floor hides the blood well enough.

A few minutes later, Rio's back. This time he's in a crisp white shirt, the first few buttons open. His vest hangs over one arm as he talks.

"So what's the deal with Lana? Are we keeping her up here?"

"You'd want that, you dirty old dog," I say, watching him over the rim of my cup.

He smirks, but there's a thread of something darker there. "She's been in my head."

That doesn't sit right. My brother doesn't let women get in his head. Not since... well, not ever, really.

"Greta!" he calls.

She appears in the doorway almost instantly. "Yes, Mr. Boar?"

"Our guest doesn't have any clothes," Rio says. "Buy her a little bit of everything." He orders. "And tell her I expect her in the boardroom in an hour, serving drinks. And you'll see to it."

"Yes, Mr. Boar," Greta says, then leaves without another word.

I drain the last of my coffee, setting the cup down. "Already? You won't give her the morning to rest?"

Rio straightens his cuffs. "She'll have to pay one way or another for staying here, right?" he grins, then checks his watch.

I watch him head back to his room for the final touches on his suit.

I should leave it there. I should let him deal with whatever's brewing in his head about her. But my mind's already replaying last night, the way she took us both, the way she said she's done this before, fuck, I'm gonna have to do something about my morning wood.

RIO

Sol's bulk fills the doorway of the boardroom like a slab of concrete. He nods at me, silently confirming that everything is according to plan.

Inside, the team of four I'm meeting are already seated, two founders, two suits from their legal team. They've got the look of men who are trying not to look nervous, hands folded neatly on the black marble table, eyes flicking between each other instead of meeting mine.

Amateurs.

The room itself does the first half of my job for me. Black marble floor to ceiling. No windows except for the glass wall that overlooks the club below.

"Gentlemen," I say, voice smooth. "Welcome."

They stand automatically, unsure if they're supposed to shake my hand. I move toward the head of the table, the largest chair by far, broad and armed like a throne and sink into it, leaning back, claiming the space.

"You've met Sol," I nod toward the door.

One of the founders, who's in his mid-thirties, clears his throat. "Yes. He showed us in."

"Good." I lace my fingers together on the table. "Now we can talk about why you're here."

The second founder, the one with that tight, over-rehearsed posture, jumps in. "We, uh, we sent over the proposal–"

"I read it." I cut him off. "And it's a decent start. But you and I both know numbers on paper don't mean shit until they're put to work."

There's a flicker of discomfort. They weren't expecting me to strip the niceties this fast.

I glance toward their legal team. One's a man in a slate-gray suit, on the fat side, sharp-eyed, watching everything. The other looks like he's been sucking lemons since birth. Both have laptops open.

I lean forward, resting my elbows on the table. "You're asking for an investment. You want our money, our connections, our reach. That means you don't just get the cash, you get us as a partner. And that partnership only works one way, we hold the majority."

Founder number one shifts in his chair. "We were thinking more along the lines of forty-nine percent."

"Fifty-one." My voice doesn't rise. It doesn't need to. "Non-negotiable."

I let the silence hang for a moment, watching them shift in their seats, before I speak again.

"Someone will be in soon to take your drinks order," I say, keeping my tone casual, almost polite.

The man in gray studies me for a moment, then leans to whisper something to his clients. They nod, exchange a look.

Founder number two clears his throat. "If we agree to fifty-one, we'd want assurances."

"You'll get them," I say. "And more. But I'll tell you what you won't get, the illusion you're still running the whole show. You bring us in, you answer to us. You work for us. You try to work around us..." I crook my head, and let the sentence hang, the silence heavier than anything I could finish it with.

As if conjured right this moment, Lana steps in, her hair a little messy, damp, falling loose over her shoulders. She's clearly just come from the shower. And then there's the dress, one of ours. Black, low plunge halter neck mini, with that flippy hem skater dress, which doesn't leave much to the imagination. She's wearing it with heels, long legs bare, the outfit almost too much for morning light.

Which tells me one thing, Greta didn't get back in time with the clothes I told her to buy. And if Lana's in that uniform... it means she's got nothing underneath it.

Every man at the table stops talking. Hell, they stop breathing. Their eyes snap to her and stay there, drinking her in, the negotiation temporarily obliterated from their heads.

I lean back in my chair.

"Gentlemen," I say, my voice is low and amused. "Please... take everything she offers." The words hang there, deliberate, edged with meaning they can't quite place. But I know exactly what I'm doing.

As I speak, I slide my hand under the table and press the discreet button built into the armrest of my chair. There's a faint hum as the air system kicks in. Not just air conditioning, the special air. Infused, calibrated, tested. Designed to loosen the edges, to nudge inhibitions until they fray. It works wonders for any woman crossing the boardroom's threshold.

She smiles, slow, easy, and her eyes find mine like we're the only two people in the room. The first breath of the cooled air hits her, carrying just enough of that chemical bite to stir something in her. A loose strand of her hair flutters across her cheek in the breeze, and she tucks it back, a tiny movement that somehow feels like it takes up the whole room.

The founders are staring at her like she's the answer to every problem they've ever had. The lawyers are trying to remember why they're here. And me? I'm sitting here with a smirk I can't quite hide, knowing I've just shifted the entire balance of this meeting without saying another word.

They're frozen. Every last one of them. Like statues caught mid-movement, waiting for the air to un-stick time. Lana steps between the two founders and leans in over the one on her right. A curtain of damp hair slips forward, a few curled strands dangling near his cheek, close enough that if he moved an inch, they'd brush his skin. The low plunge reveal her perfect breasts, bouncing freely in front of him.

She tilts her head just enough to catch his eyes through those strands. There's something depraved shimmering in her eyes right now, something hungry and unashamed.

Her voice is the sound that sinks into the space between your ribs and makes you feel it in places you shouldn't. "What do you want?" she asks, and it's not just a question, it's a lure. A baited hook wrapped in velvet. She could talk about anything.

And fuck... I feel it. That pull. My cock aches again, even though I already had it dealt with, twice this morning. But she's standing there with her breasts swaying just inches from his face, the fabric of that halter dress doing nothing, nothing, to hide the shape of her nipples. Hard. Pointed. Pressing against the thin fabric like they're straining for attention.

The founder on the other side of her isn't even pretending to keep his eyes up. His gaze drops, greedily locked on the curve of her ass, the bare skin that flashes when she shifts her stance. And the lower she leans, the easier it is for him to see what I already know, that she's not wearing panties.

A little fox.

The man under her shadow swallows hard, his Adam's apple jerking. His voice, when it finally comes, is barely more than a stammer. "Uh... c-coffee, please."

Pathetic.

Her smile deepens, not wide, but enough to show she's caught every single flicker of his reaction. Then she straightens slowly, letting that skater dress move freely over her curves.

And the room... Christ, the room is different now. My negotiation just became a hunt. Not for me. Not for them. For her. And she's already winning.

The other one, the cockier of the two, leans back in his chair like this is his boardroom, like he's earned the right to test limits here. His hand moves under the table, smooth, practiced, slipping between Lana's legs as if the act itself is nothing but casual conversation.

And from where I'm sitting, I can tell he's found exactly what he was looking for. Probably dipping into the slick proof of her arousal. Because she is aroused, I see it in the way her nostrils flare with every breath, in the way her pupils are blown so wide there's barely any green left to see. She closes her eyes, lips parting slightly, and that expression... Jesus. It's like she's feeding on the sensation, letting him stroke her in my boardroom.

And yeah, I've had enough of that.

"Coffee for everyone, Lana," I cut in, my tone slicing through the haze she's building.

Her eyelids flutter open like she's waking from a dream. "Mhm... coffee," she repeats, voice low, still caught in the undertow.

"Now," I remind her, my voice dropping into the register that leaves no room for interpretation.

She obeys, turning on her heel and walking out of the room, the sway in her hips impossible to ignore.

The door clicks shut behind her, and for a beat the air hangs heavy, charged. Then the men exchange glances, little smirks curling their lips. They're not even trying to hide it.

One of the founders leans forward, clearing his throat. "W-would we... get any other benefits by giving you fifty one percent of the shares?"

I narrow my eyes. "You mean, besides the half a million I'm putting in your hands?"

"Y-yes," the other one says, the way he says it making it perfectly clear what, or who, they're really talking about. Lana. Fucking hell. Everyone wants Lana.

I keep my tone even, but there's an edge there. "Sure. You'll get all the benefits that come with the club."

That's all it takes. They both light up like kids who've just been told Christmas is coming early.

"Great," one of them says quickly, almost too quickly. "It's a deal."

We shake hands, their palms a little too sweaty, their smiles a little too self-satisfied. They think they've just bought themselves a ticket to more than money and status.

But what they don't realize, what they never seem to realize, is that the Boarpit doesn't give away its treasures for free. Not unless it benefits us.

While we're bent over the paperwork, trading pens and signatures, the door opens again.

She's back.

The founders lift their heads in perfect unison, and the look in their eyes is unmistakable, wide, greedy, almost juvenile.

Lana steps inside, balancing a silver tray stacked with coffees. Her movements are careful, deliberate, but not steady, there's a faint tremor there. She's holding herself together, but only just. I see it instantly, the exact moment her sanity falters. The subtle hitch in her breath, the way her pupils seem too wide for the light in here, and that searching flicker in her gaze, darting from face to face as if she's looking for someone, anyone, who can sate whatever's clawing at her insides.

"Is everything okay, Lana?" I ask casually as I go back to my seat, and the rest follow.

"Yes." The word barely leaves her lips. It's almost a sigh, almost a plea. Her hands are steady enough to keep the tray level, but her shoulders are tight, her chest rising quicker than it should. She's struggling to pull in a full breath, and the tension vibrates off her like static.

"Anyone... c-coffee?" she whispers, the syllables uneven, her tone dripping with something that doesn't belong in a polite offer. Her hips shift without thought, the kind of movement a body makes when it's chasing friction.

I tilt my head, let the faintest smirk curve my mouth. "Start from here," I tell her, gesturing to my left, "and go around the table, princess."

The first man she approaches, the younger founder, leans back slightly as she bends in. Her dress strains over her chest, halter straps pulling taut, and his lips curl in a way that's far too self-satisfied for a man who's about to lose majority control of his company.

He's palming himself under the table, subtle enough most wouldn't notice. I notice. And I won't stop it.

"You're gonna love the coffee in here," I tell him quietly, the words carrying just enough for him to hear. "It comes with something extra."

His brows knit. "W-what?"

I hold his gaze, mouth the word Unzip.

He freezes for a heartbeat, hesitation flickering on his face, but then curiosity and arousal burn it away. His hand disappears from view, and I hear the faint rasp of metal teeth separating.

Lana's breathing is ragged now, she puts the coffee in front of him, and seeing the glistening cock peeking from under the table, she licks her lips salaciously, and bends down, elongating her legs, and wraps her mouth over his cock. No hands, just lips. She licks the precum with her tongue, takes him in fully, bobs a few times and then she's up. Continuing with her coffee round, she takes the second coffee, and as she places it on the table in front of the other founder, she finds him already waiting on her. And she does the same. Licks her lips, wraps them around his cock and sucks him deep. Really deep. Making him groan. Then she's up again. She has a job to do. She continues to their legal team, first the one in the gray suit, whose cock it seems hasn't seen this much action in ages. She's sucking him with extra fervor, and judging by his face, he may have come already. And the last member of the legal team is taken care of. By the time she walks towards me, they are in awe of her.

I am too. My cock needs her.

"C-coffee for you, Rio?"

"Of course." I unbutton myself and move away from the table, allowing more space for her to bend down to my crotch and do her job. She leaves the coffee on the table, and the tray too before she properly leans in, and starts sucking me, her legs elongated in the heels she's wearing, her pussy exhibited like a perfect item for bidding.

As she does, I gesture to the crystal candy dish on the table, packed with condoms. "Gentleman, your benefits await."

She realizes what's happening, and her reaction is pure awe, reverent and exactly as I anticipated. Her eyes lift to mine, wide and grateful, and she starts pumping my cock with new zest, taking me throat deep, as a thank you.

"Thaaat's right, baby. Yeees... Let Daddy's friends fuck you." I push her head on my cock and cut her air supply, but only for a moment, to see how she reacts. She takes it like a champ.

They don't need to lift her dress, it's too short anyway, and her dripping cunt is begging to be fucked. It's pulsating. One by one, they're lined, cocks in their hands. The first one, large erection, enters her to the hilt, he claws her hips in place while pumping her and grunting like a pig. She is enjoying every thrust he does, and moans through her nose as she sucks me. He finishes fast, and the moment he's out, the second one slams inside her juicy cunt without waiting.

"You like Daddy's friends playing with your cunt, don't you?" I stroke her hair as her whole body is jerking from the fucking. I push her head down on me, the gagging sounds she makes are music to my ear. "Thaaat's right. Take me aaaall in."

The guy fucking her barely makes a sound. He hastily stills inside her, exhaling, and then pulls out. Lana looks at me with her lips glossy, and wanton eyes. "Daddy... Is it over? Are they finished?"

I stroke her hair, nearly losing it when I hear her calling me Daddy. *Is she for real?*

"Two more to go, baby. They want you, and they want your cunt. Can you take them for me, princess?"

"Yes. Mmhm." She bobs her head and I try not to come before everyone finished their fucking. She's whimpering while she's sucking me, it's the sweetest sound she makes.

The third one, who I see is as thick as Brox, groans as she enters her without waiting. The moment he does, I sense Lana's orgasms rippling through her body. I pin her head down on my cock, and her eyes bulge before I let her breathe, I want her to have the best experience of the moment.

"Do not bend your knees, baby. I want you like this, bent over me, your ass up, open for them."

The girthy one finishes soon after and it's the last one's turn now. He slaps her cunt with his cock a few times, dips his cock inside, and then slowly, expertly, he slides it in her ass. I can tell it's her ass because she's shaking, her legs bucking and she perks her ass as much as she can. Then she reaches behind her with her hands, grabs hold of her ass cheeks and holds them open for him, all the while her head bobs on my cock. A sight to behold!

His fucking is the pinnacle Lana needs. She's flying and moaning while he growls and rams into her ass over and over. Finally, and too fast I think, he stills inside her but not before he reaches under her and pinches her nub, making her whimper for a long time.

With everyone finished, and exhausted, the party is over for them. Satiated, each of them spruces up while Lana is a mess of sweat and orgasms. Perfection to observe.

I pull her up and kiss her. "You've been a good girl, princess. You did good. Now go."

CHAPTER 8

BROX

"Greta! Greta!" I sure hope she's out getting clothes for Lana, because I can't be seeing her wearing that skater mini dress any longer.

Sol brought her back up here, and she's been such a distraction. She found her way around the apartment, and went straight for the fridge, carrying that lustful need on her face. She pulled a bottle of water and drank it fully, with some of the water dribbling down to her low-plunge dress. Then she looked at me, bit her lower lip and frowned as I ordered her to shower.

God damn. Rio's not giving her space to adjust. But fuck that, why do I care. I want to fuck her, too. I'm rock hard, I've been hard ever since I laid my eyes on her. So, while sitting on the sofa, in the middle of the living room, I unzip my pants and free up my cock.

"Lana, I need you here. Now!" I shout.

She appears from the hallway instantly, as if she was waiting for me to call her. Her body is wrapped in a short towel, her hair wet, too many water droplets falling down on the marble floor.

"Y-yes?" she softly inhales, her eyes half-lidded. This girl seems insatiable. Or maybe I am.

I show her my cock, and as if she's in a trance, her towel drops to the floor and she comes to me.

She fists my cock at the base and squeezes the shaft on every upstroke, she's determined to make me feel the same urgent need that's wreaking havoc in her body. I chuckle, I'm enjoying Lana a lot more than I should.

Without waiting she straddles me, and her breasts suddenly appear in front of my eyes. I latch on them, sucking the nipples and biting them, she needs it. I know. By the sound of her whimpering, I know how much she's enjoying herself.

Her only comprehension of the world at this moment is to ride me. That's her aim. She lifts up and tries to insert my cock in her cunt. I'm big, and so she lowers onto me slowly. I know the first few times is painful. She tries nevertheless. And as she groans, I grow bigger.

"Easy, sunshine. Breathe."

She digs his nails into my shoulders, and with her hand positions my glans at her entrance. Bobbing on my cock softly a few times does the trick. From the arousal, I glide in, push into her, her pussy stretching to my sweet size.

"Theeere you go," I softly praise. "Good girl."

She wastes no time. She rides me, easy at first, becoming adjusted to my girth. She raises her hips, and perks her bottom out before she slides on me again. Her movements are slow and measured, but soon she picks up speed and swivels sideways with her hips, rubbing herself on my base, taking me with her on that flight to heaven. She tilts her head back and gives me access to her nipples, and I suck them as she surrenders to the moment.

"Brox.. I-I'm flying.." she moans.

I dig my fingers into her flesh, hold her hips with both hands, and start pounding her from below. She is too horny, correction, I am too horny to let her do everything. Fuck, I never want to let her go.

"Well what the fuck do we have here?" Rio is somewhere in the background. I'm lost, you'd think I'm the one who's on drugs.

Lana's seen him and instantly she takes over the rhythm, she rides me, her boobs swaying in front of my face, all for show, for him.

Rio grabs a handful and massages it before slapping her face.

"Go on, princess, tell Brox who you will be sucking now." He unbuttons his pants and frees his cock in her face.

"You, Daddy. You!" she doesn't wait, she wraps her lips around him and takes him deep. No gag reflex.

I'm shocked, and in awe. It usually takes months before our pets want to call us Daddies. It's psychological. It puts them in their place. It makes them little, helpless, needy, and we satiate every need of theirs.

"We hit the jackpot with this little whore, Brox!"

She bobs her head a few times on him before he tangles his fingers in her hair and pulls her away. Lowering his lips to hers, he devours her needy mouth. "Lie down, sweetheart," he mumbles at her lips. "Daddy needs a fuck."

From a sitting position of me leaning on the sofa, I slide sideways and end up lying on the sofa. Still fucking her. I will never stop fucking her.

I pull her down to lie over me, and she follows, but she still rides me, not stopping at all. Rio's knee is on the sofa, on one side of me, and he positions himself behind Lana. He starts rimming her ass. Fuck, the music of her voice could make a sinner believe in salvation. He edges in, I see him pushing into her, slowly, but relentlessly, I sense him getting in halfway.

"Fuck, this is how I want my whores, so fucking wet, we don't need lube," he says, as he gains more traction, while I fuck her cunt, I do not stop. She'll learn to take us both in one hole, soon.

Rio edges his cock the last few inches into her ass and she's becoming euphoric. She bucks into him. Her mind seems hazy from so much thrusting, so many sensations at once, and for fuck's sake, I don't think I'll last.

"Your ass is so tight, baby." Rio growls. "We're gonna have to do something about that."

"Yeees, Daddy. I want that." She moans and turns around, agreeing with him all the while riding me, and being fucked by Rio. *Could we really be this lucky?*

Rio enters her fully, with a rhythm that's working alongside mine, making her body vibrate to a different level of orgasmic pleasure.

"Yeeees!" Rio growls. "Now be a good girl for me, and lie there, let your Daddies have fun."

Rio wraps his arm around her waist for leverage, and starts pounding into her, while as a good little girl, she's listening to his every word.

She goes into a wild whine, probably going through many orgasms at the same time, her whole body starts shaking, and I can't hold it anymore. I growl before I still, my cum pumping inside her without end.

"That's right, Lana, that's right, princess, you're doing a good job. That's it. Milk me." Rio is still fucking her into oblivion while her wild eyes are fixed on mine. She whimpers as I press my lips on hers, devouring every little sensation she exudes right now.

"Fuck, fuck, *fuck!*" Rio growls, and he's done too. He stills inside her, I sense him pulsating through her cunt for a few moments.

"Good girl." He pulls out and slaps her ass cheek. She's served her purpose, no doubt about that.

LANA

After so many years, my body betrays me again. But this time in a structured, debauched way.

I never liked in High School when all the boys were making a train to fuck me, without no consideration for my body. But today, in the boardroom, it was different. I was flying when Rio soothed me as his work friends fucked me from behind. I liked it a lot when Rio, Brox and I fucked. Twice. God help me, I liked it. The heat, the rush, the way my body lights up, it's awakening the devil inside me. It clings to me like smoke, curling into every thought, and I hate how much I want it back. I know it's wrong, filthy, dangerous, but my skin aches for more. And that's the part I can't comprehend.

Having a Daddy? Somehow that makes it feel less like falling and more like being caught. Tucked away.

I'm inside a bedroom that isn't mine, under a ceiling taller than any I've seen before. My room smells like eucalyptus and new fabric.

When I got back to my bedroom, Greta had already ran a bath for me, with too many rose petals floating in the water. By the time I was done, she had already filled the wardrobe with clothes for me.

Everything folded neatly, silk slips that slide like water through my hands, cotton tees cut just right, many cropped, skirts, dresses, jeans, everything. There were perfumes lining the vanity, creams and makeup I've only ever seen behind glass are now mine, or whatever "mine" means in a place where nothing is paid for with my money. Toothbrush, hairbrush, body brush, there are so many ways to tame a girl.

I move to the mirror, the tall one that makes me look like a full-length version of myself. My hair is still damp from the bath, blond waves darkened at the roots. My eyes look back at me like they know something I don't. Greenish yellow, like a lioness, looking feral.

Greta left a silk robe for me. It cinches at my waist and drapes smooth over my hips. My body has always been a question in other people's eyes, one I stopped trying to answer long ago, and instead learned how to listen.

After what happened last night, and again this morning, contraception is the only thing I can think about. Dr. Morales had been on my mind all day. I almost asked for her, and then, like someone had read my thoughts, she appeared in my room.

She was attentive, posing all sorts of questions, and when I asked her about contraception, it seemed she had come to see me for that very reason. As she laid out her instruments, she went over the choices but kept steering me toward the arm implant. Then her tone cut sharply, "You need it." The antiseptic stung, and a moment later something slid beneath my skin. I would have gone for the arm implant willingly, but the way she did it left me uneasy.

I sit on the edge of the bed, leaning on pillows as hefty as me. My legs tucked under me, still trying to figure out what's the deal. Are they coating me in gifts before they push me under? Am I being fattened for the market? To be sold?

Brox and Rio are… something. The memory hits me in hot fragments, hands, heat, a voice low and steady in my ear telling me what I am, what I'll be if I keep being good.

I should be ashamed. Instead, I'm aching, with phantom warmth under my skin where those hands were.

Get it together, Lana.

Greta left a glass of water on the nightstand, with a lemon slice drifting inside. I take a sip and scan the room. The door is unlocked, the windows are floor-to-ceiling, with a view that steals my breath, my wardrobe is a small department store. The vanity offerings are laid out for me to enjoy.

Maybe they think I'll crack and tell them.

I don't know that, but what I know is that I haven't had sex in more than three years. Not since I decided to move my focus from being a helpless girl to being in charge. But 'being in charge' is what brought me here.

And in the last twelve hours I moved through the night like someone winded me up and let me go, a nymph, a girl who remembers for a few blind minutes what it is like to stop bracing.

Back in school, God, I hate how my brain goes straight there, nurse Gemma took me aside and told me that my hypersexuality is what every young woman goes through in their youth. Because at the time, all the boys in my High School loved me, in their own way. All at once. But now, at twenty-one, I should be over it. It's what nurse Gemma assured me.

"Daddy," I say aloud, testing the word against my tongue. It feels ridiculous and right. It feels like surrender with a safety rail. Having a Daddy, someone to draw lines in the sand and soothe me when I'm close to losing my mind, makes the chaos make sense. Terrible logic. Perfect solution. My brain calls it dangerous. My skin calls it home.

I step lightly, barefoot out of the bedroom in my new summer dress, the marble floor waking me up with its coolness.

I'm starving. I'm going to ask Greta for food, but I see Jo next to the elevator, balancing three shoe boxes against her hip, and a shopping bag cutting into her elbow.

"Leave them by the door," Greta appears from the hallway. "I'll put them away."

Jo blinks. "By the door... for whom?"

Greta doesn't bother answering.

"Hey, Jo." I greet her with a smile, and step close enough to see the gold stamp on the top box.

"For you?" Jo's eyes flicker from the boxes to my bare feet. The surprise on her face curdles fast into something sour. "You've got to be kidding."

Greta's unamused. "Thank you, Jo. You can go."

Jo doesn't move. "I didn't know the shoes were for her."

A flush burns its way up my neck. "They're just shoes," I say, trying to sound casual. My voice betrays me by being too soft.

Then she smiles bitterly and narrows her eyes. "Don't worry, honey. I was once staying here, too. Then they threw me down below, under the club, like a used rag. Give it a day or two."

Under the club? I swallow.

Greta's tone turns iron. "That's enough."

Jo lifts both palms, mock-innocent, and sets the boxes down with a little too much care. She leans in, her voice low just for me. "Enjoy them before they sell you to the highest bidder, penthouse girl.”

Suddenly, my eyes snap to the elevator. The air changes, and I know it’s not a draft. It’s a presence.

The hallway darkens by a degree as Brox steps into the living room, black tee, black slacks. His eyes go to my bare feet first, then climb, slow, until the corner of his mouth ticks like he just remembered a favorite song.

“Jo,” he says without looking away from me. “Why are you still here?”

She straightens. “Brox, I–”

“Did I ask for your narration?” his voice drops. “You deliver. You leave.”

Jo’s chin lifts a single notch. “Greta asked for–”

“Leave.” He doesn’t let her finish.

Greta doesn’t flinch. Jo does. The elevator seems to swallow her as she backs into it.

Brox turns fully to me, and chuckles.

“Barefoot?” he says with amusement. “That won’t do.”

I glance at the boxes. “I have options now.”

"You do," he says, already crossing to the kitchen. "Have you eaten? You must be hungry."

"Maybe a little."

He grins. "Sit."

The kitchen looks like it belongs in a magazine for people who never spill. I slide into a bar stool at the black-marble island, the dress smoothing under me. From this angle I can see the whole living room, the long slant of the windows, the sea below.

Brox picks up a tablet, taps, and speaks into the air like it answers to him. "Seashell platter. Oysters. Crushed ice. Lemon, mignonette, the good horseradish. Two minutes." He sets the tablet down, steps behind the island, and opens a bottle of a very cold white wine. "You ever done oysters the right way, Lana?"

"The right way? You eat them. I think."

He chuckles as he pours me a glass of wine, and pushes it toward me, then he rests his forearms on the counter, coming down to my height. "Oysters are a ritual. A promise you put on your tongue." His gaze drops to my mouth. "Drink up."

I do. The wine is crisp and flinty, it steadies me.

Greta glides in with a silver tray, two dozen oysters glitter on crushed ice. She places it between us, sets down lemons, sauces, tiny forks. "Anything else?"

"We're good," Brox says, and waits until she's gone to lift the first shell. He tips it toward me so I can see the brine.

"Rule one," he murmurs. "Don't chew it to death. Let it tell you where it came from." He brings the shell to my lips, and I can feel the cool wet porcelain of it kiss my skin before the oyster slides onto my tongue, salt, metal, a shock of cold like a wave hitting mid-thigh. I swallow and my eyes flutter closed without my permission.

When I open them, he's watching me like he just learned a secret. "Good girl," he says. He takes one for himself, and I see his throat working as he swallows it.

I force my voice steady, I must ask him. "Um, the 'pets' in here..."

He doesn't even pretend to misunderstand. "Yes?"

"W-where do they live?"

He chooses a lemon, rolls it under his palm. "Different floor." The knife flashes, cutting into the citrus.

"That's not an answer."

"It's the only one you'll get."

I stiffen. "A-am I one of them?"

He looks me over, slowly. "Yes." Then he adds, "You're in your trial stage."

"Jo said you threw her down below like a used rag."

His jaw ticks. "Jo talks too much when she's forgotten who feeds her."

"Am I going to be thrown down there, too?" I hate how small I sound. I hate that I need him to say no. "What would happen if I don't pass the trail stage?"

"Eat," he says, picking up another shell. "You're gonna need your strength later."

He tilts the next oyster in my mouth, and I let it slide over my tongue. I swallow and notice him watching my throat like he owns it.

What would happen if I didn't pass the trial stage? And what does that mean? I have to be better? Worse?

I sit back, the bar stool's footrest catching the arch of my foot, and I straighten my leg and let my toes find the inside of his calf. He smirks and swallows another oyster.

"You're feeding me," I say. "I should return the favor."

He narrows his eyes, he's not sure what I'm doing. I trace higher with the side of my foot, over his slacks, a slow sweep up the line of his shin to the muscle above his knee. He doesn't stop me. He doesn't encourage me. He just looks at me like he's measuring how far I'll go without being told.

"Under the table? Creative." he smirks.

I nudge in, calves crossing, the hem of my dress sliding up my thigh as I find him again, this time with both feet. He helps me by pulling his slacks down and releasing his cock on top of them. I start playing with him and add pressure which clearly makes him grow.

"Careful, sunshine," he murmurs. "You start a fire, you don't get to walk away from the burn."

The elevator makes a humming sound and we both turn. The doors open and Rio steps out, jacket over his shoulder, shirt open at the throat, tie loose. His gaze flicks from the platter to my bare feet braced against Brox's thighs, and cock, to my face.

"Join us," Brox says without looking away from me.

I don't move my legs. I don't look down. I hold both of their eyes and try not to think about Jo's warning.

Brox slides another oyster toward me, his knuckles brushing mine as he tips the shell. "Open," he says again, and I do.

CHAPTER 9

BROX

I shuck the oyster clean and hold the shell over Lana's lips.

"Open," I tell her.

She does, and it slides into her mouth, her eyelids flutter. I feed her a second oyster, touch her chin with my thumb to make her swallow slow. She's learning how I like it, letting me pace the meal, letting me watch. Her toes keep massaging my cock under the island.

"Lunch," Rio says, amused, setting the jacket on a bar stool. "Or a lesson?"

"Both." I spear an oyster with the little fork, bathe it in mignonette, and let him see the angle of her lean toward me. "It looks like Lana here, wants to take charge."

Lana's smile flickers. Her foot stills.

Rio's brows lift a notch. "How so?"

"Look at what she's doing right now," I say. I don't look down; I don't need to. Her toes curl, undecided. She's holding my gaze, waiting to learn the rule.

Rio turns the full weight of his attention on her. It lands like a hand. "What made you start this, Lana?"

She swallows. "I-I was saying thank you."

"Well, Lana, we decide who says thank you and when. Is that clear?" Rio scolds her like a little child.

"Remind me, Rio, what do we do with girls who want to take charge?"

"Of course, we punish them." His answer is easy as breath.

Lana's throat works. "I-I–"

"What's the matter, cupcake? You don't want to be punished?" I ask, gentle on the surface, but she feels the right energy all right.

"Um, no." Her voice frays. "Please don't send me back."

Her eyes gloss over, I can virtually taste the edge of her fear.

I tip an oyster to her mouth again. She accepts it without touching me, without moving her foot another inch. Good girl. She's breathing like she just remembered there's a right answer to every question here and it lives in our mouths.

Rio takes the bar stool opposite her and steals one of my lemons. He watches her a beat longer, then nods to the hallway. "Go to your room."

She startles. "Now?"

"Now. Rest until tonight. There's a client, a high roller, I want you to serve. You'll do as you're told." He says it like he's reading the weather. "Greta will bring you something to eat later."

Her gaze skates to me, searching for a softer sentence. I give her nothing of course. She needs to learn. Especially with Rio. She stands, smoothing the dress, and scuttles barefoot across the marble. At the corner, she glances back once.

When she's gone, Rio palms an oyster, tips it, swallows like a man who doesn't flinch at anything. "You're indulging her."

"So are you," I say.

He smirks, but it's quick, wiped away by a more practical glance at the tray.

I lean back on the bar stool, pull my cock inside my slacks, still feeling the dent of her toes. I let that ghost of heat remind me she's got a brain under all that.

"Jo came up earlier," I add as I pass him an empty glass. "Ran her mouth. Told Lana where we're keeping the pets." I look at him. "What are we doing with Lana, Rio?"

Rio's jaw flexes. "Jo's jealous because she remembers what windows look like from up here."

"That's not an answer."

"It's a delay." He pours himself wine, enough to wet his mouth. "Let's see how tonight goes. Then we send her where she belongs."

"You won't be able to let her go," I warn him.

He sets the glass down without drinking. "And you?"

I shrug. "Fuck if I know. I want her here for the time being."

We're quiet for a length of time that would make most men sweat.

Rio breaks it. "Jo overstepped."

"I agree," I say.

He rests his thumb against his lower lip, thinking.

I load another shell, drown it in lemon, and hold it toward Rio. He ignores it, so I eat it myself.

"We're getting soft," I tell him. It's the damn truth.

Rio gathers his jacket, strides into the elevator, and lets the doors seal him off on his way back to the office.

RIO

Tonight, the club is quiet. Not in the people's sense, but in the 'concerns' sense. There is only one. And right now, I'm watching her from the office above the club.

Lana is at the bar, wearing her uniform, one I've chosen for my pets, for so many obvious reasons. Black halter neck, low plunge, skater hem that flares when she turns. Her hair is loose, I like her more that way. She keeps pace with Diego, he slides trays onto her palm without a word. She's good. Fast. Useful.

Just as I think he's late, the front doors at the far end open and in spills money in tailored suits; Jack Crawford, the news mogul overdue for retirement, swaddles in belly first, face creased and confident, and a trail of twelve men who orbit his gravity. They don't head for the bar. They cut straight for the west corridor and the etched letters above the double doors - Black Chamber. It's from where they always watch his latest documentary.

I'm already moving. "Brox," I say into my cell, eyes tracking Jack's shoulders through the crowd. "Our high roller just walked in with his party."

"On him," Brox answers. "Room One. Cinema set up."

I cut down the side stairs, skirt the edge of the floor, and step into the corridor before they do.

"Mr. Crawford," Brox shakes Jack's hand at the threshold. "Room One is ready. Screen is queued to your latest production."

Jack smiles the way only men who never hear no do. "Thank you. Let's see what we've made."

They disappear inside as I make my way to the bar. My cell buzzes in my palm one beat later.

Brox: Settled. They're waiting for drinks and girls.

I pocket the cell and catch Diego at the bar, already piling a silver tray with tumblers and bottles.

"Two girls," I tell him. "Maya and Noor."

"Copy," he says, then he looks past me. "Lana, grab this set for Room One."

I pivot. Lana is already there, hands out. For a second, the world slows the way a fight does right before the punch. The tray lands on her palms, she centers it with a tiny shift of her wrist, and I'm so close to yanking it back. I don't. I force myself to remember, I don't make scenes in front of my own staff. I just warn them.

"Diego." I look at him, black daggers would slice him up if my eyes were weapons.

Diego reads my face and immediately turns around and yells. "Noor. Maya!"

They appear instantly from the changing room, rushing to serve the drinks. They know what they're doing.

My cell buzzes again. It's Brox: Make sure you send Lana.

The fucker.

Diego pulls the tray from Lana's hands and gives it to Noor. "Room One," he says to her. Both Noor and Maya walk off without a thought, while Lana's eyes flick up to mine, then to Diego, clear, wondering what just happened.

"You got drinks for me, Diego?"

Why did he have to underline her name? For fuck's sake!

Diego looks at me, and I wish I didn't nod at him. But of course, I do. I'm not going to make any girl special in my kingdom. That's how mutiny happens. They're all here to serve us.

"Here, take this." He puts ten glasses on her tray and four bottles of water. "They'll be thirsty later."

Lana moves into the corridor and the dress moves with her, obedient too. I follow far enough to be a shadow.

Room One is set in an old-style cinema. Stepped rows of leather seats that do not recline. A screen that's as big as the wall. A projection booth behind smoked glass, which we often use as an observing platform. No cup holders or side tables, because men like Jack want to pretend they're back in time.

The lights are down as I enter the projector room. His produced documentary piece has already started playing and the men settle like boys at assembly.

Lana walks in with the tray, and upon seeing her, Jack lifts his chin. "Here," he calls.

I don't think she expected this to be a cinema, so she looks confused. She's cute when she's confused. By the time her eyesight adjusts and she's seen Jack, a minute has passed. That's enough for her eyes to become heavy-lidded, her lips to suddenly look plumper, and partly open, and for her to start hurrying down the aisle, craving a touch.

"Gentlemen," she breathes, the word sounding like it fits in her mouth. "Water?"

She doesn't wait for them to respond. She enters each aisle, starting with the last one, which is empty. She leans down to serve them, from behind. Her breasts almost come out of her low plunge dress, as she offers each man an empty glass, which she then fills with water. Their eyes pop out, as each of their faces are stupidly close to her breasts. If they turn towards her, and some do, they could easily suck her nipples.

Once she finishes the last row, she goes down to the next, rubbing off of the knees of those that she already served, but now she's serving the men below. No one dares to touch her, everyone's waiting on Jack for the green light. That's how he chooses his girls for the night. And Jack is sitting at the front, the last one to be served.

She's sensitive tonight, I can tell by the way she shuffles between the men, making her skater's dress ride up high as she bends down, by the way she keeps her breathing measured like she's countering nerves, or a body that refuses to be ignored.

She finally reaches Jack, and he can tell she's on the verge of her abyss. He studies her over the rim of his glass. "You drink?" he asks, casually.

She glances at the other two girls, Maya and Noor, they have already slid into the laps of two men at the back and are now being groped by many while their eyes are trained on the screen. Lana looks around, she's not sure if she should do it. But she must. Yes, that's the whole point my little pet.

"Sure," she says. "Mr. Boar said you're a high roller. Maybe I'll earn a tip."

Jack laughs: the men around him laugh because he does. "Pour her something that isn't cheap," he tells no one and everyone.

She sits next to Jack, in the front row, and someone from behind passes her a glass, and another person pours the last few drops of the whisky they have.

Maya's already up, carrying the tray back toward the bar, for more. Good girl. She knows. Noor follows.

I leave the projector room and move to the side door, taking the place where I can see the whole room and not be seen unless I want to be. I want to be. I step just enough into the wash of light that touches faces and the door hinges. If she looks up, she'll find me.

The documentary rolls on, big names, maps swallowing borders, anchors speaking with certainty.

"Tell me if my little film makes me look smarter or just richer." Jack strikes a conversation, but I see on her face, she just wants to suck his cock.

She hesitates for half a second, then drains her glass and tips herself into the seat. "I don't know you," she says softly. "You could be both."

The men within earshot grin. Jack's laugh turns pleased. "You've got a mouth on you."

"Only when I'm asked to use it," she answers, and her face doesn't even twitch when she says it. I feel it, clean and sharp, my cock twitching. She's not reckless. She knows her lines.

Jack places a hand on her leg, and smiles. "Let's watch, sweetheart."

The film continues but now, there are few hands from the men directly behind her, going down to under her plunge neckline dress. Lana is still, not moving, but absorbing every single sensation she gets.

Few more minutes, and now I see four hands on her bare thighs, one hooking under her panties as she's sitting, and dipping inside her cunt. She moans, but quietly. She doesn't want them to stop what they're doing because everybody's quiet and watching the show. Not being able to control herself, her head falls back, and she spreads her legs as much as she can, all the while sitting in her seat, and wearing her high heels. Looking like perfection.

The room's attention shifts, one by one, from the screen to Lana. It's not leering, it's gravity. Men drift toward heat. Most are up and in front of her now, the one behind lean forward.

Jack unzips his pants, puts his hand on her head and gently guides her on his cock. "Come, let's use your pretty little mouth. Show me what you can do with it."

This is the moment Lana had been living for these past ten minutes. She drops the glass on the floor, takes him in and sucks him like a lollipop.

He presses her head down on him, but allows her to take over, enjoying her bobbing up and down, his face a bliss a sixty-year-old man could have in this situation. All the while everyone's hands grope her as much as they can. They've taken off her panties, which I'm not happy about, but I've never stopped Jack and his buddies from doing what they want to do. And she is there to serve. Half of them have unzipped their pants and are waiting for her to finish off Jack before she turns to them.

"Superb, sweetheart," he lifts her head with both hands, and makes her turn to the front, where seven or eight hard cocks are getting pumped in front of her face. "Now show *them* what your mouth can do."

Her lips are wet, glossy, red, and her tongue out is exactly what they want.

The men closest to her sniggers and slaps her face, once, twice. "That's a gooood girl."

Fuck, I'm horny, I'm gonna cum just by watching them.

He tangles his hand in her hair and thrusts roughly into her mouth a few times before he stills inside of her with a deafening groan.

"Yes, you're doing great, honey," Another man is now fucking her mouth, a few next to him patiently waiting for their turn by jerking. He pulls out and ejaculates in her mouth, and she swallows everything.

"Next!" he yells.

The men line up, fucking her mouth, cumming in her mouth, over her face, tits, her dress is ruined with cum. But fuck she is the prettiest woman I've seen in a long time. Cum suits her.

Everyone has had their turn fucking her mouth, groping her, and fingering her, and I know how desperately she needs a cock, but she needs mine. Or Brox's. It's psychological, really. She needs to be fucked by her providers.

Maya and Noor didn't come back, Brox must have stopped them from coming.

Everyone's finished with her, and they're now dressing up, strengthening their pants, finishing their glasses of whisky, celebrating their production. Lana remains in her seat, her hands on her breast, playing with her nipples. Her mind, fuck knows where.

I stand in the doorway's dim wash and let her see me. Just enough. Her head turns, as if her name were called. She finds me. I nod once and her shoulders loosen a fraction. Her smile is small, but I see the need she has, vast.

"That's enough for now," Jack announces. "I got what I came for."

He stands, and the room does, too. The men gather their jackets, and their cells as Brox opens the door wide for them. He's standing at the threshold, and I move to meet him. We become two points on a gate they pass through.

Jack catches my hand in both of his like we've been working the same angle for years. "This is service," he says, and his voice carries for his men. "Privacy, pace, respect. You're running a church, son."

"Happy congregations, come back," I tell him. "We aim for habit."

He squeezes my hand, and leans in. "This one is my favorite so far."

Of course she is.

One by one, his men file past, with handshakes, nods, thanks. A couple of them squeeze Brox's shoulder like he's the one who delivered them from their sins. He doesn't even bother to smirk. The door hushes shut on the last suit and the room exhales.

I look inside, Lana's in her seat, but now she's rubbing herself slowly. Brox is already striding towards her. I follow.

Lana looks up when our shadows break over her. The smile she gives me is small and happy, and a little dumbfounded.

"Stand up," I tell her.

She does. I begin to unzip her dress and notice her melting under my touch. Brox is already at the side ensuite, pouring warm water into a jug. He takes two clean, soft clothes and passes one to me.

"You did well, princess." I tell her and dip the cloth in the water.

Her eyes sparkle as I softly begin to wipe her face. Brox does the same, we're taking care of what's ours, just like looking after a pair of shoes. If you wear them in the evening, they'll get all dirty and nasty from the use. Of course you'd clean them afterwards, you want to make sure you can use them again, and again.

"You kept them happy, for much longer that we thought you could." Brox praises her as he's rubbing her breasts clean.

Her eyes flicker up, from the praise, and probably from the sensations. "I tried to do my best."

"Yes, sunshine, you were such a good girl for your Daddies."

She deserves so much more than what we give her, and with that thought only, I get carried away and start cleaning between her legs. I cannot wait a moment longer without tasting her.

Brox reads me like a book. We make an easy perimeter, I'm in front of her, and Brox behind. I pinch her chin lightly. "You gonna let your Daddies take care of you now?"

She nods, glancing at both Brox and me. "Good."

Brox wraps his arm around her waist, "Lean on me, cupcake."

I take one of her feet and put it on the armrest of the cinema chair. The high heels she wears are wicked, and standing like this, open for me, nothing can stop me from tasting heaven.

Besides, I want to see what mine tastes like.

I kneel, and start kissing her inner thigh, closing in on her cunt, as slow as I can possibly do. She's leaned fully on Brox, and she moans as I slide my fingers inside her and rub her nub, repeating the motion, until she tightens around my fingers, and her legs buckle. "Daddy!" she cries.

Rush of cum dribbles out of her divine cunt, her hips jerk up into my hand as she rides the waves of pleasure. She feels so fucking good.

I lick my soaked fingers. Pure joy. This is what I'm talking about. She's like a threshold I can't stop crossing.

I see Brox unbuttoning his pants and freeing his cock. Fuck, if I were him, I'd be doing the same thing. He fists his hand around it and pumps a few times. Like a beacon, Lana's hand flies behind her and her fingers wrap around him.

"You need your Daddies, is that right, Lana?" I blow on her cunt and inhale as she looks at me from above. Her plump rosy lips parted, glossy, her eyes lost, as Brox kisses her neck, lost in her scent.

"What do you say, hm?"

"P-please, Daddy." She breathes.

That's all I need. I press the flat of my tongue against her cunt, soaked with arousal, from right below her legs and lick up to her sweet nub. I thrust my tongue in, I lick, I pull, I bite, I suck, I'm devouring her as she's flying, and that's the idea.

That taste, that scent, she has been sent to us by fate. We've started collecting pets at The Boarpit so we're not distracted by women, and have them at the snap of a finger, because our needs are different, and we know what we want. Legally or not. But we've never had anyone like Lana. She's insatiable, she hasn't stopped wanting. Like a goddess of sex, needy, waiting on me to thrust my tongue inside her, as horny as the first moment she entered the Black Chamber.

I pull back, and see Brox rubbing his cock on her cunt, dips in her arousal, and he starts to ease into her ass. This is my sigh to wake the fuck up and ram this whore like she deserves it. She was a good girl tonight, and good girls get fucked by their Daddies like whores.

I stand on my feet, unbutton in a maddening rush, freeing my cock fully out, and hook my arm under Lana's lifted leg. I lift her up, and she wraps her other legs around my waist and her arms over my shoulders and on my back, clawing with her nails, pulling my body close to hers with urgency, and she moans again into my mouth. I devour her mouth as I fist my cock a few times.

She's wet and ready for me as I edge inside her, an inch at a time. I hear her moans, I know she wants me in one go, but Brox is here too. I lift her by the butt cheeks as Brox's stretching her slowly already.

"Yeeees, my cumcake, Daddy's fully inside." He groans.

Her sweet cunt is so tight, she'll make me cum before I want to, and judging by Brox's sounds, he too has lost himself in her ass.

"Now this is how you make your Daddies happy," I growl as I find my place inside her.

Brox and I start pounding her, lifting her up and impaling her on our cocks, fast, feral. Wordless grunts tear from all of our throats as we slam into her, each thrust is rolling into another. I want this to last forever. But too soon her grunts become staccato as we pace ourselves to her rhythm, although it's too late. The way she's milking me with her screams is my undoing. And I know Brox. His growling tells me he's finished.

She unravels in my hands, and I release a loud, guttural groan as I empty my seed into her just as her cum gushes down my cock.

Spent and out of breath, Brox gently pulls out, and sits on one of the chairs, while she remains in my hands, grinning, with my cock still inside her. We're out of breath, panting, and she's grinning.

I'm completely smitten by her, but Brox's clarity comes faster than mine when it comes to looking after our pets. He sees the water on the table and jumps to pour a few glasses for us.

"Drink," he tells her. She does. Her throat tilts, her eyes close as she gulps every drop.

He takes a glass for himself and drops down on the chair as he finishes it.

Our eyes meet and for the first time, in a long time, I smile without being angry about something.

"Hungry?" Brox asks her.

She nods. "A little."

"Kitchen," I tell him. "Tell them to send up real food. No bar scraps. And get Sol to bring a dress in here. She needs clothes to leave this room."

Brox moves to the door, and speaks to Sol. He's outside Room One, one of his jobs is to always watch the door where we are. He knows the gig.

"Are you comfortable?" I ask her, knowing she is naked, and impaled on my cock. Which has gotten hard again.

Her cheeks go faintly pink. She grins and nods.

"We'll get you sorted in a minute."

BROX

Greta appears in the doorway with a tray, steak sliced clean, roasted potatoes, greens, a second glass of water, a cloth napkin folded into something prissy enough to make me grin. Greta catches the grin and pretends she doesn't.

"Thank you," Lana says.

We stand while Lana eats. Not over her. Near her.

We took her to the penthouse, because I made an executive decision and decided Lana worked hard tonight, and she's had enough. She needs to rest. Rio agreed with me.

She's sitting on the sofa in the living room, eating politely while I answer three messages, refuse one meeting, and tell Sol to put eyes on the east exit for an hour. Rio leans on the wall and watches her.

Even when there's more food left than I like, Lana sets the fork down. "I had enough," she says.

"More later," I tell her. "You'll need your strength in here."

She smiles, and wets her mouth, eyes cutting to mine like she wants to tell me something. But decides not to.

"Come on," Rio says, pushing off the wall. "Let's go downstairs."

"And Lana?"

"She stays here." He says.

Just as I'm about to protest, I want to stay here too, our eyes lock when we hear the elevator doors opening and someone walking in.

With us not being at the Club, Sol is spread out thinly, so someone must have gotten through the security of the building. Which, unfortunately, is not ours to manage. Even with owning six apartments in this building, there are other people who live between the penthouse and the basement. They're not a concern, they're padding, so we let them be.

"Mr. Sorrentino." Greta announces in a subtle way.

It's fucking Valentino.

Rio's jaw ticks, then stills, the way it does right before he kills. Behind me, I hear Lana gasping.

"Evening, boys," Valentino says as he's approaching us. The corner of his mouth lifts when he notices Lana sitting on the sofa, with a tray of food in front. "Heard you're building an empire here."

I smile without humor. "Brick by bloody brick."

His eyes cut to Lana and back. "So I see."

He steps into the room, slowly, measured, he knows we're moments away from killing him. He's been a burden for way too long.

"Did they tear down your house already?" It's wishful thinking, but I can't help it.

"Not at all." he says.

"Then what do you want?"

Valentino's gaze warms. "Just came to try the new pets in your pen."

I shift half a step, now standing between Lana and him. Rio does the same.

"Relax, boys, I'm only here to talk."

"Then talk," Rio growls.

"I brought you news," he tips his chin. "And a debt to collect."

"For whom?" I ask.

"The Puccini's."

"Lana, bedroom." Rio orders. She has nothing to do with Valentino, or what he has to say. Without complaining, she runs down the hallway.

"Lock the door, honey," Valentino yells, his words edged with mockery.

CHAPTER 10

RIO

Valentino takes three slow steps toward the bar and lays his palm against the marble.

"Will you offer me a drink?" the ends of his mouth crook.

"What's the news." I'd pull my gun on him if I had it. He's lucky I left it in the Club earlier.

Valentino's smile doesn't move. "I came because I'm fond of both of you." He glances at the bottles. "Though a drink would oil my tongue."

"Say what you came to say." Brox growls.

He walks, unhurried, to the center of the room. When he speaks, he corners us without taking a single step more.

"Virgil wants the girl dead," he says softly. "He wanted it then. He wants it now. He will want it tomorrow. That part isn't new. What's new is why."

No one says her name. Not him. Not me. Not Brox. The name vibrates, anyway, a wire we all hear.

"Why," I repeat.

"Because she's hiding something big." Valentino's eyes move to Brox, then back to me. "And because what she's hiding is his."

My jaw ticks. "Hiding what."

"I don't know."

Brox's hands got into fists. I keep my face still.

"Someone called Mateo is involved," he adds and inclines his head. "You see, I can be useful, too."

I don't give him that.

Brox's voice drags low. "You said debt."

"Yes." Valentino finally looks at the bar again as if the refusal has annoyed him under the skin. "Virgil wants proof the girl is dead." He savours that word. "I told him I would handle it. But he wants proof." Valentino's mouth tugs, amused by a private thought.

"He asked for either a recording, or a personal attendance. He wants to be convinced she will never resurface." His eyes touch the hallway that leads to the bedrooms. He doesn't move his feet. He doesn't have to. "I came to collect what I promised him. The girl."

Brox's face goes flat. Mine is colder. "You came to collect," I say, tasting the word. "From me."

"From you." Valentino's calm never slips. "From both of you. Families keep families out of wars they don't need. Now I need the girl."

Brox steps closer to him. Not aggressive. Not yet. But closer.

I look at Valentino. "Lana is ours."

There. Her name is said.

"Ours," he echoes mildly. "A strong word for something so new."

I take a step forward, erasing the distance he gave himself. "She's our pet now. And if I were you, I'd keep my mouth shut about her whereabouts." I look at Brox, and then I glance back at Valentino. "You want a message to deliver? Tell him she's dead."

Valentino considers. "And what if he doesn't believe me?"

"He will if you tell him the truth," I say.

Valentino's brows lift. "Which is?"

"By being here, she's already dead, anyway."

The line lands between us, heavy and clean. I mean it. I mean it because once you're inside my walls, the person you were ends. You're either remade into something that can live here, or you're disposed of. I'm not a kind man. I don't pretend to be.

Brox breathes out through his nose, the sound of a fuse burning short.

Valentino gives me the slowest nod. "It's a beautiful line," he says. "A little tragic. A little true."

"You done?"

He watches me for another heartbeat, like he's deciding whether to move one more piece.

"I am." He slowly turns on his heel and heads for the elevator. The button is pressed, and as soon as the doors open, he steps into the elevator.

I never saw Valentino as a threat. Him slipping past security used to be luck; now it's craft. He's upgraded, learned the latest tech, and walked into my penthouse like the security system was a broken app. There's no one at the door downstairs, but even so, getting up here should be harder than that. *Fucking asshole.*

I head to Lana's bedroom because Valentino is not wrong about Virgil.

"Rio." Brox's voice is a warning.

"I know." I stop at the hallway, at the line of shadow that points to the bedrooms. The door to hers is shut.

I knock once because I'm civilized when I want to be. Then I open the door because I'm not when I don't.

She's on the bed with her knees up, she looks up fast, eyes big. She's changed into a white top and jeans.

"Come outside," I say.

She rises without arguing and follows me to the living area. Brox doesn't turn when we enter, but I watch her watch him.

"What's wrong?" she asks.

"Valentino said Virgil wants you dead because you're hiding something."

Her mouth parts and then closes. She breathes through her nose once, sharply, like she's bracing for the burn of something. "I don't know anything."

The sentence is clean, rehearsed. My teeth grit.

"Try again," I say.

She squares her shoulders. "I-I told you. I saw Virgil kill someone."

Brox turns then, just enough to see her face. I don't look at him because I know what's on his, patience in a pressure cooker.

"Lana," he says quietly.

She keeps her stare on me. "And I ran. That's it."

"Who is Mateo?" I ask and wait.

She looks at me, her eyes welling up with tears, and out of nowhere, she starts sobbing. "Mateo is..." her voice wavers. "Mateo is my friend," She sobs. "Was my friend."

"Did Virgil kill him?" I ask.

She nods. "He tortured him for hours before he killed him." She weeps. "It was gruesome, he pulled his nails and...and...." Lana places her hands on her face, and sobs.

"What, Lana?" Brox is listening.

"T-they skinned him alive." She cannot stop herself now.

"And what did you do."

"I-I tried to run away, and he caught me." She sobs.

"What did he want from him?"

Her eyes flash and there it is, a small ugly flicker of truth. I could reach into that and pull her open. I could. But if I do it gently, she'll think this is mercy. It isn't. It's triage.

"I dunno." She gives a small shrug, sniffling.

"You're telling me you watched Virgil torture your friend, and you didn't hear what they wanted?" Brox's voice is ice.

She keeps quiet, holding out as long as she can. Why the fuck!

"Well?"

At last, her silence breaks. "He was asking Mateo for the drugs. He kept saying, 'Where is it? Where is the coke?'"

She won't meet our eyes. Afraid we'll catch the lie?

"Well? Where's the coke, Lana?" my patience is fraying.

"I don't know!" she meets my eyes with defiance.

"You don't know??" My brow arches, and something inside me goes very still. I give a single nod before turning to Brox.

"Take her below."

The words land like a verdict. Lana jerks, a tiny step back, eyes cutting to the hallway as if she can outrun us.

She stares like I've struck her. "You said... I won't go– "

"Until you decide to tell us everything, you'll stay exactly where I put you."

Brox doesn't move immediately. I feel his refusal like static. He looks at her, at me, back at her.

"Below," I repeat, not raising my voice. "Your rightful place."

Lana turns to him then, finally, like he's a life raft. "Brox."

He closes his eyes for a beat and when he opens them he's made of steel and inevitability. He walks to her and stops at a distance that could be mistaken for courtesy. He doesn't reach. He doesn't touch. He just lets her see that he will if she makes him.

"Come on," he says.

She tucks loose hair behind her ear and walks. Brox falls in step, a shadow half a pace back. At the elevator, she hesitates like maybe she expects it to refuse her. It doesn't. It opens as smoothly as it did for Valentino. She steps in. He steps in after her.

I move back to the bar because that's where my hands won't shoot anything I care about. I pour a drink I don't want, and I don't taste it going down.

In the basement, the club beats like a heart. Below that, there are rooms that aren't on any tour. We call it the kennel because humor softens a blade. It's clean. It's secure. It keeps what we can't afford to lose in one place so we can control what happens next.

Valentino is right about one thing, I don't need Virgil at my door.

I finish the drink and set the glass down without any noise at all.

My cell buzzes. A text from a number with no name, a camera feed unpausing. The corridor below, the door to the kennel opening. Brox's shoulders filling the frame. Lana in front of him, stiff, but shaking where she thinks it doesn't show. He says something I can't hear. She stares him down, then steps inside. The door closes. The lock engages.

I don't believe in coincidence. I believe in choices. I believe in pressure. I believe in what people do when you put both in a room and remove the oxygen.

She'll talk. Everyone talks. The only open question is how many pieces I have to break her into before the words come out clean.

LANA

I wake with my own breath clawing at my throat and the taste of iron behind my tongue. It's been like this since they brought me here two weeks ago. The nightmare isn't a dream, not really. It's a replay. A loop with jagged edges that cut me new every time. I see Mateo. I always see Mateo.

I watch them torture my best friend.

That night, I heard everything. The scrape of metal on metal. The snap of gloves. It played the same way in my head, first the quiet, then the wet sounds, and then the screaming.

They went for Mateo's hands first. I didn't need to see the gestures to know what they were doing; the timbre of pain has its own language. Nails levered up and yanked free one by one, the sucking pop of flesh letting go, the hoarse catch of breath that comes a second before the throat finds the scream. Then the tempo changed, and I understood in a way I could never explain that they had started on his arms. Skinned him. Peeled the life off him like it was a thing they could unbutton.

I pressed my mouth to my knee and tried to breathe through cloth. Hiding in a box saved my life, or so I thought. I counted the beats between Mateo's gasps, as if numbers could keep me from drowning. Remembering unwillingly all the reasons why I stepped in. Because he promised me med school money. Because I let myself believe him. Because it made me a passive observer of the power dynamics at street-level operations. It wasn't chemistry, not really. More like sleight folding into white, the powder cut with baking soda until no test could tell the difference.

When they got bored, they found new instruments. Pliers. Teeth coming out with tiny cracking sounds, like ice breaking in a glass. His voice crescendoed until it scraped the ceiling and then fell, and I thought, please let him pass out, please let him fall so far inside himself he can't feel. When the nail gun started, short, percussive thumps and a noise I'd never heard a person make before. I knew he had collapsed. I tell myself he died then, because there are limits to what a body stays in.

And somewhere between wishing I'd never agreed and hating myself for every gram I touched, I choked on a sob I'd been holding so long. What escaped me wasn't a word but a whimper, small and desperate.

They heard. And I ran.

The box split around me. I was out and running in the warehouse before I had plan. They came after me, a streak of terror chased me down two blocks in the night. I hit the squat we shared with Mateo so hard, my shoulder bounced off the doorframe, and I thought I'd made it.

But Virgil's buddy had me in his shooting range. He could have killed me. He should have killed me. It was Virgil who stopped him.

And somehow, I ended up here. In this … godforsaken place.

My cell has no windows, it's all concrete, drain grates, and cameras all over. The air is damp and chilled, smelling of mildew. A single bed is welded into the wall, a toilet squats in the corner, and a tray slot in the door.

The part that matters, the part that defines me here, are the chains. My arms are shackled high, bolted into the wall, the iron heavy enough to bruise. I'm kept tethered even when I sit on the bed. And when visitors come, the chains are pulled tighter, turning me to face the wall and I end up on my feet, stuck to the cold concrete. Exposed. Available.

Ten men a day. Sometimes twenty. Sometimes thirty. I've stopped counting, because numbers mean nothing here. They arrive at random, footsteps echoing down the corridor, the lock jolting open. Their hands are cold, rough, and eager. They laugh sometimes, whisper other times, and they always fuck me. Some want to violently fuck me, some to spank me, pour hot wax over me, and some want to spread cream over me, glossing my skin as if my body were some kind of exhibit. They smear everything across my breasts, my thighs, my ass, rubbing it in until it shines. Sometimes they linger, jerk and sometimes they do a quickie, and run out. And then they leave, and I am left sticky, glistening, breathing hard in chains that never let my mind find peace.

And the worst part, the part that gnaws at me like teeth in the dark, is not the fucking, the brutality. Not even the humiliation. It's the unpredictability. They come whenever they want. Random. No warning, no rhythm. I never know if it will be one man or twenty. I never know if I'll be left alone for hours or seconds. My body craves everything, all at once, in a storm that would burn me out. Instead, it's scattered, fractured, leaving me raw with wanting more. The anticipation drives me insane.

The air here is different too. More ragged. Empty, like a lung collapsing. Upstairs, in the club, the rooms are scented with sweat, and sex. And probably something addictive. Down here it's something else, thin, soured, a cold draft seeping from the vents. And yet, despite it all, despite the brutality and the hunger and the way they use me, I find myself enjoying it. I hate that truth, but it's the truth, nonetheless. My body hums after every visit. My skin longs for the next hand. My mind coils with need.

I've been kept in solitary confinement ever since Brox brought me down here, two weeks ago. But at the times when I have no visitors, through the small slit at the hinge of my door I can see the larger space where the other girls are kept. Chain-links, cots, bolted tables.

Dr. Morales runs the show here. She told me I had to earn my food, my clothes, my place. But I'm still being fed amazingly well. I'm given any clothes I want, but that doesn't matter because they get torn from my body all the time.

The other girls talk to me through the crack sometimes. Jo was the first to gloat.

"I told you, didn't I?" she sang through the metal. "Penthouse girls always end up down here. Cute how you thought they'd keep you upstairs."

I didn't answer.

"Did they let you keep the robe? Did it smell like them? It won't help you here. They'll forget your name in a month. I'll help them."

Maya is different. "You're not the first," she said one night when the lights dimmed. "Dr. Morales isolates the ones with stories. Makes it easier to wipe them fully from you."

"What was your old story?" I asked, though my voice sounded strange to me, like it had forgotten how to be human. I have only been hearing my own moans in my cell.

"No story. I had the chance to run away, but I didn't. Rio and Brox look after us if we are good. They always do." A pause. "Dr. Morales is the asshole."

Dr. Morales is part of the terror. Hair scraped into a bun, white coat sharp as her voice. And this morning, I saw her in close up. The lock jolted, and she stepped in.

"Good morning, Lana," she said, like she was making hospital rounds. "Lucky day."

"Every day is lucky for me in here." I answered with irony. I'm not hostile. I've never been. I'm full of love that has always had to be tamed.

"A client asked for you," she continued, writing in her pad before looking up. "Someone you met before. At the cinema event." She curled her mouth. "He and his friends would like to host you."

"There'll be more than one man?" I smiled sarcastically. "Oh no!"

As far as I was concerned, as long as I was not sent back to Valentino's or to Virgil's, they could do anything they wanted to with me. It almost felt like luck, finding someone with the same kink as mine, if I believed I could ever be lucky.

"You will eat now. You will shower. You will dress. You will rest until you are called. You'll need your strength." And then she added to the man behind her. "Unchain her."

She snapped her fingers, and as they left, a tray slid through the slot. Steak and potatoes.

Without the chains, my arms felt so much lighter. My whole body too. I ate. I took the shower she wanted me to take, then dressed in the lingerie she left for me.

I lay on my back and watched imaginary constellations on the ceiling where damp discolored the paint. Every patch is an island. I named one Mateo and let myself cry without noise for a few minutes. Then I turned my face toward the door and breathed slowly.

I'm half-asleep, when I hear the lock click again. It's Dr. Morales. She looks me over, then she nods to the camera.

"Come on." She orders.

The hallway outside is narrow, white, lit with strips of flickering fluorescence. Every twenty steps, a camera, its red dot steady and watching.

Dr. Morales is in front of me, her low bun doesn't have stray hair. She stops by a glass door and lets me pass. "I'm going up to here."

I ignore her and continue walking to the stairwell. I remember this hallway.

I notice the air shifts, it's lighter now, better quality, for sure. I inhale deeply, this is my peace.

At the top, the door waits for me to open it.

CHAPTER 11

BROX

The Black Chamber breathes like an animal tonight. The hum of air conditioning is low enough to slip beneath the skin, seeded with the Boarpit's little advantage.

The observation booth in room four is why we chose it for this client. I lean my shoulder against the smoked glass and stare at her.

Lana.

It's been two weeks since I haven't had her sweet cunt. It was tough. The toughest thing I had to do. But I promised Rio.

And he had to promise me, too, that he would not go and visit her down below. It was tempting, fuck was it tempting.

He thought Lana would break if every ten-fifteen minute someone raped her, fucked her, played out theirs kinks on her, but she didn't say one word. She moaned though. And that was the perfect porn channel for two weeks that we got hooked on.

She steps inside with a small hesitation, and I don't think I'm ready for what I see. Black heels elongating her perfect legs, black lace lingerie that clings to her like it was designed for her alone, an open cup bra, matching garter belt, and panties with open crotch, trimmed so thin they barely exist. Her hair is loose, spilling like the sun over her shoulders. She looks breakable and proud all at once, and I know that's a contradiction, but fuck me if I don't feel it. Her lioness eyes just glance at the dark glass and I feel like I've been seen.

My jaw tightens in anger immediately. She should be next to me, and not in a room, by herself. Especially when I haven't seen her this close for so long.

Fuck knows how long Rio would make her stay down there if one of Jack Crawford's men didn't request her. We haven't agreed fully on the price yet, but he wired the money, and it cleared instantly. The same amount Jack paid. Someone who wanted her, no doubt about it.

But if they hadn't ordered the other two girls from that night, Noor and Maya, I would've shut the whole thing down.

Just as I think about them, the side door opens and Noor and Maya glide in after her. They offer Lana a smile that carries more pity than joy.

One thing that's good is the air there. If they were anxious before, I'm certain now they're not.

"Come on, let's set up the space." Maya starts. "Bend down here, arms stretched out in front of you."

Lana is confused and Noor quickly helps her.

"No, Lana, I'm here, you're on that table, over there, and Maya will use this table, next to me."

There are three sleek steel tables bolted to the floor, each with a padded edge, each one outfitted with discreet little rings welded on the side back legs. Lana bends down on her table, and Maya fastens a leather belt across her waist, tight enough to hold her bent, then slips the cuffs over Lana's wrists, chaining them to the little rings on the side legs. I notice Lana's wrists are purple and make a mental note to do something about that.

Noor submits to the same treatment without question.

With my cock twitching I should look away, but I ignore it.

Maya finishes by bending down on her table, and that's when Sol enters. My second-in-command is methodical, almost reverent, as he secures Maya in place the same way. Then he moves to the wall on their blind side, unfolds the wooden partition, and locks it into place.

I know this design well, three neatly cut round openings lined with leather, set at the right height for men who want to conduct business with their cocks while they talk numbers.

On this side of the partition, the girls' cunts and asses are presented. Offered like a buffet. On the other side, he secures their heads in place, and they become holes with a face. Exactly how these clients like it.

I know Rio is watching, too. I can feel him through the surveillance feed, even though he hasn't joined me yet. He'll be thinking the same thing as I am, no one should've been able to request Lana.

Sol is happy with the whole set up and slides the doors open.

Two men in masks step in.

Both wear an angular mirror mask, light scattering off the facets like broken glass. The only way to tell them apart is by their ties. One has a suit with a red tie and the other with a black tie.

They take their seats at the table across from the partition, and the sound of folders opening, pens clicking, papers aligned, fills the room. Not once do they lift their masked faces toward the women waiting, bound and bent, because of course, this is business first, and pleasure second.

Their conversation flows in low voice, they talk about shares, three companies, three investments, three potential acquisitions. One must go. One must be cut loose to strengthen the rest.

While they talk about which investment bleeds too much cash, the Red Tie unzips his pants and helps himself with a condom from the table. Then he squeezes a dollop of lube hanging on the side of the partition wall, and he claws Maya's hips as he enters her. The girls are by now in so much need, they need both men working them. Not one by one.

The Black Tie follows suit by doing the same. Noor moans before he enters her which is always the perfect song to my ears. But Lana, as she hears the girls moaning, being fucked, the grunts of the men, I see her arousal starts dripping down her legs. She's restless, she moves from one heel to the other.

Red Tie moves to Lana, but as he knows how needy our girls get, his hands move idly, he's spreading lube across her butt cheeks first. Lana flinches as cold lube slicks her asshole and cunt, but she welcomes it, as she's famished for cock.

Red Tie edges his cock in her ass, while she moans. Slowly, long, loud, and then she bucks a little backward. Wiggles with her hips. I haven't seen this done by any other of my pets. Red Tie groans, and starts grunting as he fucks her hard, like a pig, his nails are dug deep in her flesh as he holds her in place.

And my nails are dug into my palms until crescents burn. I should be in there with her. Rio and I haven't discussed it, but we know our rules. If she's ours, one of us is in the room. We must talk, dammit.

Black Tie is surprised at the abandon Red Tie fucks Lana, and he nods, and circles in front of them. Red Tie laughs and mumbles something about this whore being the right acquisition.

Black Tie strokes Lana's cheek, tilts her face toward him as if savoring the sound of her voice, and puts his cock in her mouth. Then he pulls it out, and lifts it up, with Lana's tongue landing on his balls.

"Suck them, whore."

She licks and sucks his balls until his cock grows to its full length.

"Gooooood girl. Now.... say aaaah!"

He slaps his cock against her face, over her forehead, her cheek as she's pounded in her ass by Red Tie.

Maya and Noor whimper, they can't touch themselves because they're tied, and these two assholes are focused on Lana a little too much.

Black Tie tangles his fingers in her hair, and starts fucking her mouth, faster and harder. Then he rams her a few more times before stilling inside of her, groaning as he empties his seed deep into her throat. She swallows every drop, just like a good little girl that she always is.

Rio storms in the observation booth, slamming the door behind him. "I don't like this," he mutters.

"No shit," I growl.

"I couldn't verify their names," Rio adds. "That's a problem."

I lean forward, my eyes locked on Lana. "Look! Lana's petrified."

Red Tie cums with a grunt, too, and says something I can't catch, too quiet for the mic. But then he laughs loudly, a sound I know too well.

It's Virgil.

It's like the air pressure drops out of the booth. My vision narrows, black creeping in from the edges. My hand goes automatically to the Glock at my hip. Rio's drawn his gun, his eyes blazing with fury.

Virgil pulls a blade, shining under the dim light, and heads to where Black Tie is, wanting Lana's throat.

I slam out of the booth. Rio is already ahead of me. We crash through the side door, with our weapons raised, my whole world reduced to the red haze of rage.

The girls scream as we storm in. Maya jerks against her restraints, and Noor twists violently, but it's Lana's gasp that cuts me open. She's still, frozen, as Red Tie, or Virgil, has come to her head and is dragging a knife along her skin.

Rio doesn't pause. *No one touches what's ours.* He fires, and the bullet tears through Black Tie's head. The mask shatters off as blood and brain matter explode across the partition. The body crumples before it knows it's dead.

My hands clamp on Virgil, wrenching him back, but he's too fast. His knife slices my forearm, shallow but hot with pain. I snarl, slam him against the wall so hard the plaster cracks.

"Thought you could walk into my house, you piece of shit?" I roar.

He grins through his bloody teeth. "She's a great fuck, you know!"

Rio fires again, the bullet punches Virgil's shoulder, spinning him half around. Another shot, lower, and Virgil staggers with a wet groan, blood running down his arm.

Still, the bastard's moving. He lunges for the wall, slamming his palm onto the emergency lever. Our hidden exit slams open with a metallic shriek, smoke flooding in fast, choking. We set it as a deterrent for others, not us.

I fire blindly into the smoke, bullets ricocheting against steel. No hit. By the time it clears, Virgil's gone.

I whirl back. Lana's eyes are huge, glassy with terror, but she's not screaming. She's shaking so hard, her restraints rattle. She's staring at me like I'm the only thing keeping her alive.

Rio's fury boils over. He raises his gun and empties the clip into the dead body, each shot cracking through the room, making the girls shriek.

Then, as cool as he could be, he cuts the cuffs off Noor and Maya, shoving them toward the exit. They stumble out, sobbing, grateful just to be released.

But Lana stays.

I cut her free. Her wrists are red, raw from the cuffs. She sways when she stands, and presses against me, trembling like a leaf, and I catch her before she falls.

"You're safe now," I murmur.

Rio wipes blood from his cheek, his eyes locked on me over Lana's head. He doesn't need to say it. I already know.

We have a problem.

I lift her into my arms as she clings to me. She's pale, damp with sweat, her pulse racing under her skin.

Rio holds the door for us. "Penthouse," he says. "Now."

"Pass me the tablecloth, I don't want to draw more attention to her."

Rio pulls the tablecloth from the table and covers her.

I carry her out of the Black Chamber, her breath feathering hot against my neck. The club noise fades as we ascend toward the one place above it all.

RIO

It was harder than I ever thought, keeping her down there. Every night and day the monitors lit up with her chained to the wall, arms pulled taut, waiting for whatever bastard I sent in next. And I didn't look away. I forced myself to watch, because this is the price of control. But it ate at me, each arch of her body, each moan, it looked like everything but not for what that cell was built for – breaking people.

The fucked-up part? Half of me wanted to tear the doors off their hinges and drag her back upstairs, lock her away from every hand but mine. The other half knew I couldn't. Discipline is everything. If I show weakness for her, our other pets would get bratty. I couldn't care less if they do, but then Sol would see it, Brox too, and everyone else would follow. The empire we bled for unravels the second I let her mean more than a body on a chain. So I sit behind the camera, enduring it, punishing myself more than I punish her.

Every time I heard the chains rattle, I ground my teeth until my jaw ached. I imagined it was my hands on her, not theirs. I imagined her looking at me the way she did, like she saw the monster and didn't care. That's what made it unbearable. Not the brutality. Not the endless parade of men. But the way she glowed under it, like she was made for fire, and I was the one starving myself from the flame.

Virgil slipped through our fingers and there was nothing more we could do. I shot him twice, and if we're lucky, he's lying somewhere, dead, just like his buddy.

Black Tie was on the floor with his brains spilled all over the room, and Sol had to stay behind to deal with the body, bleach the mess, make sure no one saw or heard anything.

And Sol's men, they are good for what they are, crowd control, muscle when a client steps out of line. But beyond the walls of the club? They're not trained to track, corner, and kill. That's on me and Brox. Always has been. And tonight, we failed.

The taste of gunpowder and blood hasn't left my tongue since we dragged Lana out of that hell downstairs and into the penthouse.

I glance at her, as I enter the living room, she's trembling. She doesn't fight when Brox lowers her onto the sofa. She just folds into it like she has no strength left.

Her knees draw up. Her arms wrap around herself. And her eyes, green, wide, flick from me to

Brox like she doesn't know which one of us to cling to.

Brox's arm is bleeding badly. A deep slash along his forearm where Virgil cut him. He pretends it's nothing, but the blood is already soaking into his sleeve, dripping to the floor.

"Sit," I snap at him, sharper than I mean to. "Don't fucking argue."

He drops into the chair across from Lana, his eyes are still raging with unfinished violence. He won't admit weakness. He never does.

I move fast, I take the robe from Lana's bedroom and drape it around Lana's shoulders so she's not sitting there in lingerie. Yeah, that's still her room. Her fingers catch the fabric, pulling it tight. Her lips part, but no words come out.

"Stay," I murmur, softer now, before I head for the kitchen. "Brox, take off your shit." I yell.

I take warm water, clean cloth and antiseptic. The basics. I take from the kitchen drawer a few dermaclips for his wound. My hands are steady by the time I carry them back. Lana's eyes lock on the bowl, then on Brox's arm.

"Give it here," she says. Her voice is small, but sure.

"You don't need to lift a finger, Lana," Brox says softly, as he places the shirt on the armrest next to him.

She ignores him and takes the cloth from my hand like it belongs to her. Dips it in the warm water, wrings it out, and kneels beside him. When she presses it to his arm, he hisses but doesn't pull away.

Her hair falls forward as she concentrates, gentle but firm, wiping blood from his skin. I notice the faint red bands circling her wrists, bruises from chains that have bitten too long into her flesh. I left her down there too long.

She moves to his jaw next, cleaning blood droplets from his cheekbone.

She glances at him. "Pass me the derma clips."

Brox blinks. "You know how to do that?"

"I went to med school for a year," she murmurs.

Brox smiles through the pain. "Guess you're not just a pretty face."

Lana peels open the packet of derma clips carefully, her brows pinched in concentration. She presses the clear strip over the cut along Brox's arm and sticks it down. I see his every muscle strung tight beneath her touch, and his eyes never leave her face. Fuck, what are we going to do with her?

She finishes applying the derma clips, and goes back, sinking onto the sofa. "Are you going to send me back now?"

She catches me off guard. For a beat, I'm silent, too stunned to form a word. Then I pull myself together. I know this is the worst time to be sarcastic, but the bite is out of my mouth before I can stop it.

"You didn't like it down there?"

Her gaze lifts, catching Brox first, then locking on me. Straight. Dead on. Those green eyes pin me where I sit, pulling me into a place I shouldn't want to go, yet in my mind, I'm there already.

"It's not that. I... I want to be here with you."

Am I supposed to say something? Me too? I want you every damn day of my life?

"Then the question still stands – Where is the coke, Lana?"

We mustn't forget why we sent her to the kennel.

For a long moment, she says nothing. Her eyes glisten, but she doesn't look away, she's holding my gaze like she's weighing the cost of truth against the safety of silence. I can see the war flicker in her pupils. Her lips part once, close again. Finally, she speaks.

"In our squat. The old house. The one that's supposed to be torn down for a new building. It's in the crawl space under the floorboards. I-I was helping Mateo. Stepped the coke for him."

Um, excuse me?

"You steeped the coke?" my brows lift, caught somewhere between surprise and something close to awe.

"Why? Were you dealing? Are you an addict?" Brox narrows his eyes.

"No." She shrugs. "He promised me money for med school."

Brox doesn't say a word, and neither do I. We just stare at each other, both trying to decide what's the bigger revelation. That we found Puccini's coke, or that Lana is smart, and has real ambitions.

"So, Virgil lost Luciano's cocaine." I finally mutter, ignoring everything I learned about Lana.

"Yes! *Finally*, we can expand into that market. Fuck the Puccini, if they want it back, we'll sell to them." Brox exclaims. He's doing the same.

Before I can respond, he is already on his cell. "Sol. Listen. I need you to take four guys. Go to the squat where Lana used to live. Her address? You ran the checks on her, didn't you? Right. Figure it out. Check under the floors. You'll find something special. Bring it back here. And be careful."

He hangs up and leans back. "Sometimes fate drops a gift right into our laps." He grins and then gets serious again and looks at me. "But right now I want to find out how Virgil slipped through our vetting process. And who told him about Jack Crawford's cinema party."

"We'll find out tomorrow. If Jack is the weakest link, big shot or not, I'll find a place for him deep underground." I add. "And as for Virgil, if he's not dead already, I'll crucify that asshole, and then I'll fuck him raw with a spiked combat club."

"I like the idea." Brox pushes to his feet and heads down the hall, the cut on his arm covered with a large Band-Air. "I'm hitting the shower."

Lana shifts onto the sofa, pulling the robe tighter. Her eyes flick up to mine.

"D-do you think he'll come back for me?"

"Virgil? Yes."

Her eyes open wide, her lips part in fear.

"But not if we get to him first." My voice softens. She's had more than enough terror for one day.

"Thank you." She gives me a small smile, then hesitates, her eyes wandering as if searching for the right words. After a pause, she looks back at me. "Can I ask you something, Rio?"

I nod. My name on her lips is oddly satisfying.

"You and Brox... have you always had this kink?"

I study her. She's not mocking, or afraid of me.

"Yeah," I admit. "Since we were young. Control. Power. Sharing our pets with others is true ownership."

Her lips part. "Me too."

That makes me pause for a moment.

"The air in those rooms," she continues softly. "I noticed it's different. Better. It reminds me of how I was in high school. It's where I felt different for the first time. I had this need that I couldn't shut down. I couldn't stop myself. But there was too much judgement. They called me names. I didn't care, but after a while, it got to me," she shrugs. "And then I tried to be normal. To show less of me in the world. This is the only place I felt... free. Not judged. Like I can finally... breathe."

Something in me snaps. I see the hunger inside her, the need she's been holding down for too long, it's what I've been seeing in her eyes all this time.

She knows something's different about the air in the Black Chamber. Of course she does. How stupid of me, thinking she had no idea. There has never been a pet that didn't get mad when we told them, or if they didn't figure it out by themselves. Threats, calls to the police, fighting, until one by one, they all submit. Daddies' little pets. But Lana.. Lana took to the air, and made it hers.

I tug her robe loose. It parts, spilling lace and pale skin into my hands. My palm slides down her thigh, along the garter strap, and her breath hitches.

Then I press my mouth to hers. It's not violent, yet. Her lips tremble, and melt against mine.

"Rio..." she breathes.

"Show me your need, Lana," I whisper, my mouth brushing her ear.

Her answer is a whimper, hips arching before words catch up. "Yes... Daddy."

The word detonates in my chest. My cock strains instantly, the sharpest hunger I've felt in years. I claim her mouth harder, deeper, until she's clutching at me like I'm her only anchor.

I push her back on the sofa, climb over her, part her thighs. She's soaked already, the crotchless panties give me too easy access. I slide a finger in, sink into her heat, and she gasps so loud it echoes in the glass walls.

"Fuck, you're ready for me," I rasp.

She nods frantically, and when I open my pants and release myself, the head of my cock nudges against her, thick and heavy. She trembles, from need.

"Please," she begs, nails digging into my shoulders.

I push inside slowly, deliberate, stretching her inch by inch until she's clawing at me, lips parted in soundless moans. Her body clamps around me, greedy, welcoming, like she was made for this.

"Look at me," I command.

Her eyes lock with mine as I sink to the hilt. We both groan at the same time, raw and unguarded. I start to thrust, my hips rolling, every stroke measured, deliberate. Her hands cradle my face, and I don't stop her.

I kiss her again, softer than I should, until her thighs quake and her body arches into mine. Her orgasm rips through her fast, choking her cry against my mouth. I keep thrusting, slow but relentless, dragging her through it, until she's shaking under me.

Brox enters, I don't need to look up to know.

He's in the doorway, towel slung low, water still dripping down his chest.

Lana sees him too. Her lips part, her moan is louder, almost offering herself to both of us at once.

Brox's mouth curves.

I don't stop moving inside her. If anything, I thrust harder, showing him she's mine right now. She cries out, trembling. I have no intention of stopping, because for the first time in years, I'm not thinking about control, or empire, or war.

I'm thinking about her.

And the fact that for once in my life, maybe, just maybe, I found the right person for us.

He tosses the towel aside, his cock already thick, swollen, dripping at the tip. He strokes himself slowly as he comes closer, gaze locked on Lana.

"You've got no idea what you do to us, cumcake," he murmurs.

Her head tips back, panting. "I-I want..."

"What do you want?" I demand, teeth grazing her neck.

She shudders. "Both of you."

The sound that rumbles from Brox's chest is pure hunger. I pull Lana towards me, making space for Brox to lie on the sofa, and he grips her hips as he does. His hard cock presses against the curve of her ass.

"You're soaked enough to take me, sunshine," Brox growls, and before she can protest, he's spreading her cheeks, spitting, pressing the thick head against her tight hole.

Lana gasps, nails raking my skin. "Daddy–"

I hold her face, forcing her to look at me while my brother pushes in behind her. Inch by inch, her body stretches, trembling between us.

"Breathe, baby," I whisper, stroking her cheek as Brox sinks deeper. "You know you want us both. You're ours."

When he bottoms out, she's crying and moaning all at once, pinned between us, stuffed so full it feels obscene.

We move together, my cock sliding in her cunt as Brox thrusts into her ass, a rhythm that makes her shake, scream, and beg. Every time I slam in, she clenches around both of us, and Brox grunts against her ear.

"Fuck, sunshine, you're perfect toy to share," he snarls.

Her cries break into words, desperate, breathless. "Y-yes- please, please don't stop.."

The sound of her begging drives me feral. I kiss her hard, swallowing every noise she makes while Brox slams into her from behind. She's unraveling, body writhing, orgasm after orgasm ripping through her until she's nothing but sweat and tremors.

I can't hold back. Neither of us can.

I pump into her, deeper, harder, until I feel the rush build, molten and unstoppable. Brox's growl mixes with mine as we both explode, spilling into her at once, filling her until it drips down her thighs.

Lana collapses between us, limp, trembling, moaning even as the aftershocks ripple through her.

I kiss her hair. Brox strokes her hip. And for a rare, terrifying second, I feel something close to peace.

178

CHAPTER 12

BROX

Lana sleeps on the sofa, curled up like she belongs here. Rio draped one of his blankets over her, tucked it around her shoulders like a man who actually feels something other than bloodlust. I can't stop staring at him, wondering when my brother became this softer version of a man.

She said she wanted to be with us, here, and my mind went blank. No one in this world has ever said that to us. We push people away, or we shackle them close if we want them. But Lana, she chose us. She wants us of her own free will. And that truth rattles me more than any bullet ever could.

Her breaths are shallow, steady. I can still smell her on my skin, and if I close my eyes, I can hear the sounds she was making when she unraveled between us only twenty minutes ago. *Fuck!*

Her hair's spilling across the cushion, the hem of the throw has ridden up just enough to show one bare ankle, the other tucked beneath it.

Rio's had a shower and changed his clothes. Wearing black slacks and a t-shirt, he sits at the end of the sofa, next to her feet, and every now and then, his hand drifts, stroking lightly over her ankle, her arch, like he's reminding himself she's real. It's not lust, it's something heavier. I can't decide if I'm jealous or pathetic.

I sit in the armchair across from them, in my slacks and t-shirt too, a glass of whiskey hanging from my fingers. "You keep petting her like that and I'll start thinking you want to build a picket fence." I can't help myself.

"Shut up, Brox." He's not in the mood. He takes a large gulp from the whisky in his hand and finally speaks. "Virgil's fucked."

I scoff, knowing perfectly well what I'd do if I get my hands on him. "You think?"

He doesn't rise to it. Just keeps his eyes on Lana's sleeping face, like speaking too loudly might wake her. "He lost Luciano's coke."

"Do you think Luciano knows?" I ask.

Rio shakes his head. "He must know about the coke missing, but not about Virgil's cockup. If he did, Virgil would already be a corpse. Luciano doesn't hand out second chances. What's more likely is Virgil's covering his ass, wanting to kill Lana before she can talk."

I tilt my head, considering. My brother's not wrong. "And here she is. Breathing in our penthouse. What the fuck does that make us, huh? Accomplices? Targets?"

Rio's gaze flicks to me, sharp as a blade. "Makes us the only ones standing between her and a shallow grave."

I lean back in the chair. "When did we start giving a damn about anything but the business?"

He doesn't answer. Just strokes Lana's foot again, absent, protective. It's almost tender. This new Rio, this human version, it unsettles me. But fuck if it doesn't also amuse me.

The elevator dings. Both our heads snap toward the sound. Sol steps inside, his suit jacket is rumpled, shirt collar open, sweat darkening the fabric above his sternum.

His eyes find mine first, then Rio's, then they land on the small shape under the blanket and stick there a second longer than he means.

He's carrying a black duffel. It looks heavier than it should. He lowers it to the coffee table like he's putting down a body.

"Ten kilos," Sol mutters. "Bricks of it. Pure. What the fuck are we doing with this, Rio?" his eyes dart from me to my brother, then to Lana. "What game are we playing?"

My heart kicks, not with fear, never with fear, but with the thrill of possibility. I unzip the bag just enough to see the stacks wrapped tight, white gold staring back at me.

I laugh. "Sol, we're entering the big leagues." I stand up, turn to face him, grinning. "Drugs. More money, more power, more fun. And more people to put in the ground."

Sol stiffens. "Brox– "

I look at Rio, grin sticking. "Tell me I'm wrong."

Rio leans closer to the table, careful not to nudge Lana's feet where they're pressed into the cushion under the blanket. He doesn't look at the coke. He looks at me.

"This is suicide," he says. "We're not ready for this."

"Define ready." I clench my teeth.

"You want to step into Luciano Puccini's lane," he says. "You think two brothers and a handful of bouncers can stand against the Puccinis? Against their entire network? We'd need an army. At least a hundred men, loyal, trained, willing to die for us. We do not have the infrastructure for that. We do not have the insulation for that."

"Wrong." I retort. "We have politicians in our pocket, cops on our payroll, and judges who look the other way. Every empire starts with nothing. You think Luciano was born with an army? No. He built it. Brick by brick, body by body. We're smarter. Meaner. Hungrier. This city is ours, they just don't know it yet."

Rio rises now, and Sol edges a step back from the table, "Boss," he says to Rio, "Maybe I should go?"

"Yes. Thank you, Sol." Rio nods at him.

Sol nods once, twice, eyes cutting to the sofa and back, and then he disappears the way good men do. The elevator doors close behind him.

Rio stands between me and the bag of cocaine.

"Luciano's not a man you cross. If he knows this coke is his–" He trails off.

I drain the last of my whiskey and set the glass down hard enough to make a sound. "He won't find out."

Lana murmurs, a sound like someone smoothing a crease in a sheet and both our heads turn toward her. She's right in the middle of all this chaos.

"It's settled, then. We're entering the world of drug dealing," I announce, Rio needs to hear the certainty in me, even if he hates it. "All thanks to our beautiful pet."

Rio's jaw ticks. He doesn't say anything. He doesn't have to. His stare is the answer, which then moves on to the window.

He doesn't blink. "I can't tell if this move will keep us alive... or gets us all killed."

"Virgil fucked up," I say again, sometimes you have to circle back to the truth.

Rio's eyes come to mine, steady. "He did."

"We won't."

He holds my stare for three breaths and then nods once. It's not agreement. It's not permission. It's the thing brothers give each other when there isn't a third choice to vote for.

The elevator hums somewhere far below and grows.

Lana stirs, and her lashes flutter open. She blinks, disoriented, her pupils slowly adjust. She finds Rio, then me, then the bag on the table. Her body goes tight under the blanket.

"Where... what time is it?" her voice is rasped.

"Late," Rio says, as he sits next to her. "Sleep. You're safe."

She shifts upright, pulling the blanket with her until it pools at her waist. The bruises on her wrists are dark, I hate that I notice it.

Her eyes drop to the bag, to the edge of plastic peeking out.

"Is that...," she whispers. "You got it already?"

"Yes. Ten bricks," I say proudly.

"What are you going to do with it?" she breathes.

"We'll drop a rumor on the street that the Boars are entering the market and see who crawls out of gutters."

"Do you have a lab? Or somewhere to step the coke?" she asks.

Rio lets out a low, sarcastic hum. "Hmh. A lab, Brox. Right. Are we really ready to deal coke?"

"We've got to start somewhere." He says and looks at Lana. "I suppose Lana here can help us."

The glimmer in her eyes isn't fear anymore, it's ambition. "I can help you with stepping. And with packaging."

RIO

I keep count because numbers don't lie, even when people do.

It's been a month since we got the coke. Twenty-eight days since we started pushing it. Twenty-eight days of watching Brox slam his head against the wall of Miami's east side and swear the bricks will give before he does.

They haven't.

When Brox gets angry, his brain goes on walkabout. He forgets our leverage cabinet is full, and the keys are all labeled. Ha, he thought coke moved itself. He's learning the slow way what I learned the hard way, markets don't move because you tell them to, they move because you pry away what's wedged inside people's ribs and squeeze until it bleeds.

I let him run it alone to start.

My cell buzzes on the desk, one vibration, the signal for "they're here." I'm already standing, watching the club below through the one-way glass, the dance floor, a blur of light and heat, the security team moving like a tide on the edges.

Lana's been staying in the penthouse with us all this time. She's also been working at the Black Chamber because after all, it's where she belongs. She knows what I want, what I crave, and she's learnt how to bend it in her favor. Like the time she overheard me closing a deal and pushed me to bring the associate to the club, to sign the contract in front of her. Of course, I did. It worked for me, and it worked for her, too. She feeds on that spotlight, soaking in everyone inside her body, like it's her victory all along.

But Lana's been more useful than I ever expected. Brox allowed her to handle most of the coke stepping, while Sol pulled in a few of his men to cover the packaging. But it's more than that, she's been feeding Brox tips about Miami's dealing spots, the kind of knowledge you only pick up when you've lived with a dealer and observed street-level operations.

When Brox hit a dead end with the east side crews and dropped a name, Pasqual, Lana froze. She knew him. Said if we offer her to him, with his circle, he'd sign the deal without hesitation. Turns out she'd burned him once, handed his name to the cops, thinking that would get Mateo off the streets. Since then, Pasqual's been hunting her. Mateo told her that much.

And right now, Brox is in the boardroom next door, six east side men arranged in front of him like a menu. They've taken calls from Luciano Puccini, obviously. But they took our meeting because Brox insisted.

And because Lana found a way to persuade them.

I straighten my cuffs, roll my shoulders once, and head for the door. Sol holds it for me as I step aside.

The conversation dies when I cross the threshold. Brox doesn't give anything away.

"Evening," I greet them.

They all rise halfway on alert.

"This is my brother, Rio Boar." Brox introduces me. I hear the inward sigh. He continues. "As I was saying, our terms beat Puccini's'. Hands down."

"All we've seen are the same conditions on paper." Pasqual, their leader, says. "They're not better."

"They are," I answer for Brox, as I take the head chair on the opposite end. "But before we talk numbers, we clean the air. You walked in here thinking you had choices. You don't. You have consequences."

Pasqual's right-hand man leans in, ready for a fight.

"First," I go on, lacing my fingers. "You don't do deals with Puccini while you do deals with us."

"We haven't agreed to anything yet," the one with a beard speaks.

"You agreed when you walked in here," I tell him. "But I'll humor you. Brox, tell them the benefits."

Brox clears his throat. "You work with us, your margin's fixed above street," he says. "Your routes are covered; your corners insulated."

"Thirty percent is our cut," The fat one calls, like he's daring an answer.

"Twenty-five," I correct without blinking.

The tall guy shifts in his chair. "Puccini's promised twenty-seven."

"Twenty-five," I repeat. "The Puccini will promise anything that will get them in your home," I say. "Then they eat your kids first."

A vein ticks in Pasqual's temple. "And you don't?"

"We don't kill the hand that feeds us." I let that sit. "But I'm not here for metaphors. You move our weight on the east side, you buy our protection by keeping your mouths shut."

The sixth man, who's wearing a bright red jacket, laughs softly. "And what do we get besides a threat?"

"You get to contribute."

He opens his mouth confused, and that's when Sol knocks once and opens the inner door. It's time to impress these assholes with spectacle.

Sol wheels in a bench and the space becomes dead silence.

Lana is naked, and tied on the bench, lying on her stomach with arms stretched around the bench and fastened down by the wheels. It looks like she's riding the bench; her legs open wide and fastened on the sides. Her cunt is positioned higher, and is glistening, and ready. Her head is turned sideways, lying on the padded surface, on her left cheek. Her mouth held open wide with a metal mouth spreader.

"We are a service club, and this is one of our many little sluts we want to introduce you to. Our very own cum bucket. And I thought, maybe you could all contribute. Do us a favor, in a way."

Their eyes open, but the instant distention in their pants talks for them.

All of my pets have experienced this once, but for Lana, this is her first time. Dr. Morales inserted in her vagina a thin layer of her innovative rubber to act as a barrier, to keep Lana from getting any STDs as she'll be ridden raw. My beautiful Lana. Her first breeding. Fuck, I'm so proud! And to think that she thought of it herself!

The air here is not any different, it's always the same, infused with those little maca pearls. But to be on the safe side, she was prepped downstairs, in room two. So, she is more than needy right now.

"For those of you that might know her, please be gentle, this is her first time." I smirk, and wheel her around slowly, allowing everyone to take a good look at Lana, her open mouth, her greedy eyes, her ass, and the arousal glistening on her cunt. Pasqual's eyes pop. He recognized her.

"That cunt is waiting for you, can you see the dribble down her legs?" Brox encourages them.

One by one, they stand up, get comfortable, remove their jackets, and free up their cocks. This is what connects men. The lust for little pets.

"Let me hear you say something now, you cunt!" Pasqual steps first and pushes his cock into her mouth to make it wet. He pulls out, goes around, and slides his cock in her cunt as easy as that.

Lana tugs on her restraints a little, enough to rouse him.

"You can't talk now, can you?" he pounds her while the rest of his friends already have their cocks in their hands, pumping them.

I stand by Lana's head, and Brox is still in his chair, having unbuttoned his pants, rubbing his cock.

"You gotta loosen up your ass for me, sweetie," Pasqual's moving too fast, he edges into her ass, pushing in bit by bit as she bucks and shoves until she adjusts to his size. She moans, but they don't want to hear moaning. They want her to hear restraints tugging, they want the power play.

He pulls it out, then starts edging it in her ass again. "Yeees, you feel me? Take that! Take it!"

"Pasqual, move your feet on the bench, next to her, so I get access to her cunt." The one with the beard impatiently asks him.

The tall one is already by her head, fucking her mouth.

Pasqual, steps on the bench, and makes space for the bearded guy's cock to enter her cunt at the same time. "Yeeees....." He groans while Pasqual enters her to the hilt, and pulls it out, fully, and again.

Lana is flying, her eyes roll backward, and she moans, her whole body trembling as her ass is being pounded. I see her need being quenched, and then I hear the first two being close to cumming.

I stroke her hair softly. "You can do this princess. You can do it for your Daddies."

Pasqual pounds her violently, until within a moment, he stills, releasing a guttural groan, and empties his seed into her. He pulls out slowly, allowing a few drops to roll down her leg. Then he slaps her ass hard. The bearded guy is next, now having her to himself, he grabs her hips, clawing deep with his fingers and starts to dictate the rhythm.

The tall guy shouts just as his cum spurts directly down her throat, with some ropes of semen landing on her face.

I step away, give them space.

It feels as if we're in the club as the music from below has entered the room, Brox must be on top of this.

Her whimpering can be heard over the music, because it's the sound of the angles. Makes me want to join them.

The bearded man finishes spectacularly, which gets Brox up on his feet, and waiting patiently for his turn. Pasqual's right-hand man and the one in the red jacket, which is now hanging on one of the chairs, are tag teaming.

"Let's see if this slut can take us both," The red jacket guy says, and joins Pasqual's right-hand man's cock. There is enough of her arousal, and they slide into her. Lana tugs on the restrains. And moans, she's objecting, but since that requires a bigger influx of air in her chest, it helps her, and makes both cocks slide inside her cunt with ease and fervor.

And I'm right, they both hold on her body and fuck her at the same time as she bucks in and out, needing cocks more than ever. The fat guy is not going to win any cunt space, and he is happy with her mouth.

I walk over to where her lips are fucked, and lean down.

"Be a good girl and stop moaning for Daddy." I whisper. Her sounds are driving me crazy. "Can you do that for me? Come on. Shh."

She's losing herself, her eyes roll over, as she's pounded, these two cocks are making the whole ordeal worthwhile. And they cum at the same time too, groaning, and spurting ropes of semen inside and finishing with a few drops over her cunt, while their fat friend's knees buckle as his cum shots end directly on her tongue.

The six of them are done, our cum bucked filled with cum, and she should be wheeled out, just like she came in.

I'm not sure about her, but I know my cock is fucking twitching seeing her used.

I turn to see Brox, he's been jerking, and he too, ejaculates over her ass and cunt, too, growling as he does.

"Keep this cum bucket close." He says. "We may want to use her again."

I nod at him, and at the rest of the men, and wheel her out.

First stop is for her to take a shower, then a hot bath. She needs to replenish her strength. She's proven to us as invaluable, and we want to use her as much as we can.

But not before I remove her mouth spreader and let her properly suck my cock. Because Daddy needs her too, Daddy needs her tongue, her moans, her hands, her mouth, her throat.

The BOARPIT

CHAPTER 13

BROX

Greta's cooking fills the penthouse with smells that almost don't belong here. Garlic, seared beef, the faint smokiness of wine reduced in the pan. It's domestic, normal. Except nothing about us is normal.

It's been a few weeks since the east side dealers took my offer and started moving the coke. And life has been good.

I sit at the head of the table, Rio on my right, Lana on my left. We're in the dining room, a place we rarely use.

Greta floats in and out, setting down plates before disappearing into the kitchen.

Lana's hair falls over her shoulder in waves. She looks at home here. Too much at home.

"You're quiet tonight," I say, spearing a piece of steak.

She glances up at me, as she lifts her fork. "I was thinking."

"Dangerous habit," Rio mutters, sipping his wine.

She smirks at him, unbothered. That's what gets me every time, she doesn't cower. Not anymore. She's come into herself in ways I didn't expect. We got her as a pet, chained her to our world, but she doesn't act like some meek little captive. She sits here like she belongs. Like she's making decisions for her own life, even when her life is in our hands. Maybe that's what Rio and I love most about her.

"What about?" I press.

Her fork scrapes against porcelain as she sets it down. "Once you kill Virgil... would I get to go out?"

Rio freezes mid-sip. My knife stills against the plate.

"Out?" I repeat.

"Or maybe... get a cell phone?" her smile is cautious but sly, like she's testing how far she can push. "I've been working hard for you. And in my spare time all I've been doing is watching Netflix, and I'm getting bored."

The audacity. The little fox.

"You have been working hard for you, Lana." I lean back in my chair, eyeing her. "And enjoying it too."

She bites her lip, smirk curling, but doesn't argue.

"Still," she says.

"Still?" I echo, and she nods.

Rio sets his glass down. "Oh, you want to go out?"

Her eyes flick between us. "Well, yes."

"Where would you go?" I ask, genuinely curious. "Or if we get you a cell, who would you call?"

Her smirk falters, replaced by a shrug. "I don't know. I'd watch reels. TikTok's. Scroll until my thumbs go numb. And, I have nowhere to go, anyway." She hesitates, then adds softly, "Living with you has been... better than anything I've ever experienced."

"So, you want to go out, but you don't know where you'd go," Rio concludes for her.

"Mm. Yes. But– "

"That's okay." I cut her off with a smile that makes her narrow her eyes. "I'm sure we can arrange something."

She leans forward, eyes sparkling. "You'd really take me out?"

"Yes," I say, spearing another bite of steak. "And you're gonna love it."

The table goes quiet except for the sound of cutlery. Greta returns, clearing plates, replacing them with plates of dessert, panna cotta.

Lana takes a bite, watching me. She's pushing boundaries every day, and in a wicked way, I don't want her to stop.

Rio finally breaks the silence. "You're spoiled, you know that?"

She laughs, a soft sound that shouldn't fit here but does. "Haven't I earned it?"

I smirk. "Oh, sunshine, you haven't even started earning it."

Lana's laugh lingers when my cell buzzes on the table.

I glance at the screen, it's Sol. Rio catches it too, and his brow twitches.

"Yeah." I answer.

Sol's voice crackles with tension. "Luciano wants to see you. He's downstairs in the club."

"Sure," I say, keeping my tone lazy. "We'll be right there." I hang up and force my good mood not to slip.

Beside me, Lana straightens, her hand brushing my arm. "What is it?"

"Nothing you need to worry about." I rise, pocketing the cell, and tilt my chin toward Rio. "Luciano's downstairs."

Her lips part like she wants to argue, but doesn't.

Rio pushes up from his chair. "Let's go." He glances at Lana. "Stay here. We'll be back soon."

I'm already on my feet, heading for the elevator. The ride down is slow, mechanical, every floor dragging my patience thinner. We catch our reflections in the mirrored doors, three-piece suits, collars up - we look the part. Deadly.

"You good?" Rio asks.

My jaw tightens. "More than good."

The elevator dings, and the doors slide open.

The club is not open yet, and as such, it's stripped of its usual heat and chaos.

Sol is near the entrance, ten of his men spread behind him like a wall. His shoulders are rigid, his eyes darting between us and the figures deeper in the room.

Luciano Puccini stands at the center like a king who thinks the floor belongs to him. Four of his own men flank him, thick-necked and armed. His face is red, eyes burning when they lock on me.

"Puccini," I say smoothly, stepping into the dim light. "Didn't realize you were booked for tonight."

"Cut the shit, Brox." His voice booms through the empty club. "I heard you're selling on the east side."

Sol shifts uneasily. Rio stands stone-still beside me. I take a step closer. "You heard?"

"I don't hear lies." He jabs a thick finger at me. "No one touches the east side but me. No one."

I grin, slow and cocky. "If you came here to buy my coke, I'll give you a good price. East side, west side, it doesn't matter. I'm in business everywhere."

His face darkens to crimson, a vein bulging at his temple.

"You think this is a game?" he roars. His men twitch, hands sliding toward their jackets heavy with steel. "You're nothing but pups, playing at being wolves. Step on my ground again, and I'll gut you both where you stand."

Rio's jaw ticks, but he doesn't move. He knows I got this.

I chuckle, mocking him. "Careful, Luciano. Too much yelling at your age and you'll pop something. Wouldn't want you keeling over before I get a chance to bury you myself."

The club goes deathly still. His eyes blaze, his nostrils flare, but he doesn't step closer. He knows better. He came to scare us, not to die tonight.

Finally, he spits on the floor. "You're dead men walking."

He storms out, his entourage trailing behind like shadows, leaving the stink of his rage heavy in the air.

The door slams shut. Sol exhales hard, his men shift, uneasy as though they've just survived a hurricane.

Rio rounds on me, fury flashing. "You just painted a target on our backs."

"We already had one." I'm not worried.

"This isn't a joke, Brox. He'll come harder now."

"Good." I step closer. "Let him. We don't fucking kneel. We don't march to another man's drum. We're the Boars."

Rio stares at me. He knows I'm right.

"Then we need a plan," he says darkly. "Because Luciano isn't going to stop."

"We won't either," I bark.

I look back at the empty club, the shadows still holding the echo of Puccini's rage, and feel my pulse thrum with hunger.

RIO

For the past ten days we've lived under a shadow, waiting for Luciano to make his move. Every night I expect it, an ambush, bullets through the club, but nothing comes.

Sol doubled the men on watch. We've got eyes on every corner, more bodies at the doors, patrols running shifts like a small army. Still, silence.

Brox doesn't seem bothered. He shrugs when I bring it up, shrugs when I remind him Luciano's not a man who forgets. Instead, he leans back in his chair, smirks, and says, "We've got leverage – Virgil. Stop grinding your teeth and have some fun for once."

Fun.

He looks at Lana when he says it, like she's the solution to my tension. *Maybe she is.*

She's been working for us nonstop, our clients can't get enough of her, demanding her like an addiction that only she can feed. And she still has time to unwind us after work, giving us more when she gets to the penthouse. Pleasing us isn't a choice, it's her duty, and she knows it.

She's perfection, we've been so damn lucky with her. We couldn't say no to the cell phone request. It was the least we could do. We loaded it with our numbers and checked in on her every day. She was right, she didn't have anyone else to call or text. Just us. Sometimes she shoots off a flirty little text, and before long, she had our numbers memorized by heart.

"Let's take her out," Brox said last night. "The mayor asked me to do something for the steelworkers who've been keeping his projects moving. He wants to do some kind of community goodwill."

"You mean he wants to buy their silence while the town hall's dirty business keeps rolling? Sure." I chuckled. "What do you have in mind?"

"Let's surprise them tomorrow on their way to work. Both parties would be in for a treat."

Since Brox had already thought this through, my only job was to make sure Lana's activities from last night aligned with our plans for today, starting with a visit from Dr. Morales.

Thinking about it, we haven't gone out with any of our pets before. If they're going somewhere, they're sent with Sol as their handler. Of course, Lana isn't just special; she challenges every thought we've ever had in our heads.

I pull the sunglasses from the drawer in our suite, the polished frames catching the light in my hand. Lana's already watching me, perched on the bed with her legs tucked under her, curiosity bright in her eyes.

"Greta," I call, "bring Lana's clothes."

Greta appears with the outfit we chose, a white top, snug but light, and a pleated mini skirt that barely grazes mid-thigh. Clean, simple, almost innocent. Almost.

Lana runs the fabric between her fingers, smirking. "You two really want me dressed like this?"

Brox steps in behind me, already in cream chinos and a crisp linen shirt rolled at the sleeves. He tosses his jacket over the chair. "It'll look good when the sun hits you on the street."

Her cheeks flush, but she doesn't argue.

By the time we're ready—linen, light colors, polished shoes—Lana's standing at the mirror, fussing with her hair, twisting it up into a ponytail. The sight of her makes something in me tighten. She looks... free. And fuck, it's dangerous how good that looks on her.

We take the elevator down together. The three of us in silence, with Lana pretending to study her reflection in the mirror, but her grin is giving her away.

When the doors finally slide open, we step out, the rush of street noise hitting first. The sun blinds off the glass towers as we walk out onto the pavement. Lana blinks, tilts her head back, closing her eyes against the brightness, smiling. Her first time out in months—and it shows.

It's a real smile. Pure.

She deserves this outing. But I'm certain she'll be surprised we're taking the bus.

We walk down the street, and her smile falters when she sees no car waiting for us. We stop at the corner.

"Bus?" she asks, brows rising. "A-are we taking the bus?"

"Mhm." Brox adjusts his cap. "That okay?"

Her laugh bubbles out, nervous but amused. "Sure. I've been on a bus before, ha."

"Good," I say. "Then I'm sure you gonna like it."

She nods, though I can see her scanning the street like she doesn't quite believe it.

The bus arrives with a hiss of brakes, heavy and loud. Brox lifts a hand to wave it down as it pulls to the curb.

The doors swing open. The driver squints at us, already annoyed. I step up first, pull out cash, and pay for the three of us.

"You gonna move it or stand there all day?" the driver mutters, glancing at the clock.

I ignore him. We're in, the doors close with a snap, and the bus lurches forward.

Brox and I walk to the back where there's more space, fewer seats, and a wide standing area.

"It's only a few stops," Brox says.

Lana's excitement is obvious, her eyes darting to every window, every corner, she's probably seeing Key Biscayne this close for the very first time. To her, it's a sightseeing tour. To us, yet another way to see Lana's lustful desire.

I lean on the handlebar by the window. Brox mirrors me on the other side. Lana stands between us, her hands wrapped around the overhead rail, her ponytail swaying with each bump of the road.

At the next stop, around fifty men get in. Workers, clothes stained with grease and sweat, boots heavy. They flood the aisle, talking loudly and laughing harshly.

The bus swells with heat, men pressing in from all sides.

Brox watches them. "Factory shift change." He mutters.

The back of the bus fills too. It's getting packed. Like sardines in metal.

And Lana, Lana is the only bright thing in white.

I see the hungry eyes of thirty horny men boring into her. The bus jolts over a pothole, and rough hands clutch at her, desperate to feel some semblance of female flesh.

Lana stiffens under the weight of it, her knuckles whitening on the rail. A man with rough hands presses in behind her, his palm sliding bold across her waist. He grinds his body into her back like she's not even human.

"Hey– " she gasps, jerking forward.

Before she can move, another hand reaches from the side, groping her breast through the thin fabric of her top. A third man slides his hand boldly up her skirt and firmly grips her thigh as he traces his fingers up toward her core.

The movement of the bus works in tandem with the men's actions, causing her to feel every touch and thrust intensely. Her breath hitches as one man moves a hand between her legs, skilfully making his way through the fabric of her panties.

Fuck, this is what I love. Brox was right, we had to test her outside of the Black Chamber. To see her need, her desire, to see if this little whore's wants are aligned with us.

Brox is stroking himself already. He glances at me and chuckles, nodding at Lana. Yes, he was right. She shines.

Lana's hands desperately grip the handlebar above her head, trying to maintain balance while she is subjected to the unrelenting advances of these strangers. With each jostle of the bus and each new set of hands on her body, I see Lana being overwhelmed by sensation–I hear her, her moans, the roughness of calloused fingers exploring and ravaging her soft skin as she attempts to keep herself together.

The man rubbing himself on her climaxes, leaving a warm, sticky substance on her lower back.

Her skirt is hiked up, and a sea of eager hands explore her exposed thighs, inching higher and higher. Lana's breathing becomes labored, and I know my little princess is already wet between her legs.

A man with a wolfish grin, tugs his fly down. His engorged cock springs free, throbbing with want. Lana's eyes lock with his, and she can't look away as he begins to stroke himself in time with the bus's rhythmic movements.

The man beside her presses his crotch against her leg, and I see the outline of his erection through his pants. He looks her in the eye, his expression a mix of lust and challenge, as he unzips his fly, too.

A heavyset man kneels between Lana's legs, pulls down her panties and before she can say anything, his mouth is on her aching cunt. She moans, the sound lost in the din of the bus, as his tongue laps at her throbbing arousal.

Another stranger locks eyes with her, his lust-filled gaze traveling down to her lips. Boldly, he leans in, giving her a wet kiss, his tongue invading her mouth as his hands roam her body, leaving her gasping for air.

The strangers surrounding her take advantage of her vulnerability, their hands greedily exploring and ravaging every inch of her trembling body. I see a rough, calloused finger rubbing insistently against her clit, as she attempts to keep herself together.

The air is thick with lust and sweat, and Lana gasps for breath as the bus continues to lurch forward. The men drape themselves over her like a pack of hungry wolves, each one fighting for a taste of her soft flesh. Beneath the groping hands, Lana's legs begin to quiver as the relentless fingers continue their intimate invasion. Her breathing is ragged and shallow, her body instinctively grinds against the touch that both torments and arouses her.

One of the men roughly pushes Lana against the window and yanks up her skirt. He pulls down his pants, and without a word, he enters her from behind, taking her with a primal ferocity that rocks the bus. Lana's muffled moans blend with the rumbling engine as she surrenders to the pleasure. When he finishes his job, two men turn her around and lift her, hooking their arms under each of her knees as she holds herself for the window rail. They forcefully spread her thighs, and without warning, they both plunge into her, one after the other, their cocks alternating in her soaking wet cunt. Lana's back slams against the grimy window, her grunts of ecstasy muffled by the deafening engine.

After they climax, they let a burly man have a go at her. He lifts her onto him and seats down, forcing her to straddle him. He ruthlessly impales her, her legs trembling as she tries to brace herself against the bus's shaky movements. Another one takes her from behind while she's being fucked, entering her ass one inch at a time, each lurch of the bus onward.

They hurriedly and relentlessly fuck her while she's writhing between their bodies. When they cum, they let her drop on her knees. She's surrounded by the men who deem her worthy of their use. Without lifting her head, she hungrily services them, taking one cock after another, swallowing their seed like a starved cumslut. They grope and squeeze her breasts as they each ejaculate ropes of cum over her, all while the bus drives.

With that ultimate act of degradation, at the next stop, the men get off and disperse in an unsettling silence. Lana slumps against the cold metal pole in the back of the bus, and Brox and I run to her. She's flying, being used is what tips her over all the while I'm left with the biggest hard on I've ever experienced in my life. Sharing is caring, I always say.

CHAPTER 14

LANA

I wake up to the smell of coffee creeping under my door, I lie there and allow it to wash over me, my palms on the cool sheet, my body slack in that sweet ache I didn't know I could ever have.

In here I haven't had a single normal morning. And I don't think I want normal anymore.

I think I want this, the fire and the bed after. Brox and Rio saved me, yes, but it's not just gratitude I feel for them, it's absolution.

I feel their love in a hundred small ways, in how Rio stands too close when I'm nervous in a new scene, in how Brox whispers to me sweet nothings when I work, either just when I'm about to fly above everyone else, or stepping the pure coke.

This place isn't a cage.

Every time I let men use me, every time new chaos ensues in my head, one of them is there.

After my night's work, we always play. They take me apart and put me together again. More than a few times a night. It's when I call them Daddies, because it curls something low in my stomach, and lets me surrender without shame.

And all of this would be perfect if I didn't wake up in the morning in my bed, alone. It's not that my room is not beautiful. It is, it has beige walls, white sheets, and a window seat that warms in the afternoon. All this is mine. But once in a while, I want to share it with them.

And today, it's the same again. It's morning, and I'm alone in my bed.

I sit up and swing my legs to the rug, as my hair falls down my shoulders. My body remembers their hands, mouths, weight. The soft praise that follows the storm. I didn't know I could sleep this deep, and heavy.

I walk to the bathroom, splash water over my face, brush my teeth, tie my hair into a ponytail.

When I catch myself in the mirror, I see something new in my eyes, not fear, not even defiance. Intention.

I pull on a white t-shirt and shorts and step into the hall. The penthouse opens around me like a sky with its high ceilings, the smell of fresh coffee thickening as I cross the living room.

Brox is on the sofa, in a black t-shirt and slack, barefoot, a laptop balanced on his thighs. He's working.

He doesn't look up when I appear. "Morning, sunshine."

"Morning." I smile. "Where's Rio?"

"Already gone." He taps a key, skims a document, taps again. "Gym. Walk through the club. Then meetings."

I drop onto the cushion beside him, drawn by both gravity and now, habit. He smells like coffee and that spice I've decided is just his skin and not anything you can buy in a bottle. I fold one leg under me and angle toward his shoulder.

"Can I ask you something?"

"Go ahead." He flicks his eyes to me.

"I want to sleep in your room." The words leap out of my mouth.

His fingers stop on the keys. "Do you, now?"

"Or Rio's," I say quickly, then force myself to slow down. "Look, I love my life with you. You give me something I never thought I could have, but when we... I mean, when I fall asleep with you, I always wake up in my room. And it's not that I'm complaining, I like my room. But I want to share it with you." I swallow. "Share us."

One of his eyebrows kicks up. "Us?"

"Yes." I nod.

"As in...?"

"Not like that," I say, heat jumping to my cheeks even though I do mean that too. "I mean, not just like a pet, curled up at the foot of the bed because you told me to be. I can be that. I like being that, for you, for Rio, when we want it." I breathe. "But I want more. I want... mornings. I want to wake up with your arm numb because I made it so. I want to make coffee or steal yours." I meet his eyes. "I want us in a way that doesn't end when I fall asleep."

He studies me. "I don't get what you want."

"In a way, I have two roles with you," I say. "At the club, where.. where you use me in any way needed, and in here, when I'm with you two. And each time, when we stop playing, I wake up in my room, reset, like a doll put back on the shelf. I don't want to be put back." I inhale and let it out slow. "I want to stay with you. Some nights. Or most."

His mouth curves, but he stays quiet.

I keep talking.

"And there's more," I say.

"You want more than our beds?" he's amused.

"Yes." I look at his laptop, then back at him.

"I want to take a bigger part in your business. I've proven myself with the coke, with my ideas around it, which you liked. And used. Um, I'm not letting go of the Black Chamber's work, that's for sure. But let's say, you put me in charge of the pets." I lock eyes with him. Direct.

That gets a short laugh out of him. "Ambitious."

"I'm serious."

He closes the laptop one-handed with a soft click. He turns fully, forearm up on the back of the couch, eyes slanted at me like I've just become more interesting. "Tell me what 'in charge' looks like in your head."

"I would start by firing Dr. Morales," I say.

Brox barks another laugh, this one longer.

"The only thing I'll keep from her is her innovation, the lining cream for the vagina. That's something we should patent."

"Yeah, that's a good idea." He agrees.

"She's an idiot," I continue. "She's careless in a way that hurts girls who don't have room for more hurt. She's the reason Noor fainted in room one two weeks ago."

"Noor wanted to be there. And she fainted because she wasn't ready to take that many men at that angle."

"Dr. Morales doesn't care about them. I'd have put Maya on that day. Maya is stronger. And Noor wanting to do a scene is one thing, but whether she can manage, is completely another."

Brox's gaze doesn't soften, but there's approval in the stillness there. "Go on."

"I'd hire a doctor who knows what they're doing and gives a damn. I'd set rules everyone's happy with," I say, counting on my fingers because it helps me build the thing in the air. "No forced scenes. Ever. A panic button in every room that summons Sol in under ten seconds."

He hums in his throat. "You're forgetting, pets do what they're told."

"Ha. Pets love working in the rooms. You think you make them? Think again. They need it. They crave it. How many have come back? All of them. And I'll hire more willing girls, if we need."

"How?"

"I'll talk to the women, explain what we do. Offer a trial night. The ones who stay and work for us, will be here indefinitely."

Brox licks his lower lip, thinking, "Mhm."

"Health care on our dime," I say. "And not because you're saints but because you care. Shifts no longer than three hours in the rooms without a break. And a full day off."

"Excuse me?"

"You heard me. Give them a day off. Most have nowhere to go and will stay in, but they'll have the choice of leaving for one whole day."

"And what if they want the chaos, the protection, and none of your structure?"

"Then they shouldn't be here." I don't blink. "You're keeping them on leash because of you, and your kinks. But now you have me. And I'm more than capable of looking after the two of you. And more, if needed."

"Lana, you know that makes my cock twitch instantly."

"I do." I smirk and continue.

Brox's grin shows the edge of a canine. "And you? Where do you sit in this little empire of rules?"

"By your side," I say. "Like a little puppy."

"And if we say no?" the corner of his mouth tilts.

"You need me."

He drops his head back on the couch and laughs.

"You want to sleep in my room," he says at last, voice low. "That's how all this started, right?"

"I want to sleep in your room, Rio's, or sometimes for both of you to wake up in my room." I smile. "I want us to exist beyond the night."

He studies me for one long beat, two. Then he reaches up, catches the base of my ponytail, and tugs, gentle, pulling me that fraction closer that always makes my breath catch.

"Say please."

I swallow. "Please."

His eyes flicker. "You've forgotten you're my pet."

"I haven't."

"You've forgotten how you should address me."

"Daddy," I whisper.

He releases my hair, his thumb brushing the pulse line on my throat.

"Daddy, please.." I beg.

He taps the closed laptop with two fingers, cutting my electricity off in a moment. "I'll talk to Rio."

"About?" I lost myself for a moment.

"About all of it," he says. "You in our bed. You running the pets." The grin comes back, crooked, dangerous.

He reaches for his mug, takes a sip, then offers it to me. I wrap both hands around it because it's warm and because it's his. I drink and smile and hand it back.

Then he snags my wrist, tugging me onto his lap for a second that stretches. His mouth finds my throat. His breath is coffee and warm, and my hand fists in his t-shirt as I pull him closer.

BROX

Her audacity still rattles around in my head. For asking to sleep with us, and to be in charge of our pets.

Her ambition looks like madness. She's got it, that's for sure. If she'd had the chance, she would have finished med school, too.

I'll talk to Rio about it, but not now. He hasn't slept in days, and I'm not about to pile more stress on him.

For now, I drink my coffee, which lately tastes better with Lana next to me. That is, until my cell starts buzzing.

It keeps vibrating on the table, with an unknown number showing on the screen.

"Brox." I bark into the handset.

"Brox, it's Luciano Puccini." His voice is calm, too calm. Last time we were in the same room, a spark of gunpowder was missing for everything to explode. But we got lucky, nothing went down.

"Figured we should iron out some shit." He mutters.

He doesn't appear to be hunting. He's pliant, and that's the strangest part.

"What shit?"

"Can I come over?" he asks.

"Sure." My voice hardens. "As long as you come alone."

He huffs a small laugh. "You don't trust me?"

"If you bring anyone, I'll know you came for a fight."

A breath passes. Then he speaks. "Fifteen minutes."

"Fifteen." I cut the line.

Lana's gaze is on me, her eyes wide, she knows the coke we're selling Luciano's coke.

"Stay up here," I say and see her nodding obediently.

I dial Rio's number, and don't wait for him to speak.

"Luciano wants a meeting. Fifteen minutes. Boardroom. He's coming alone."

"Alone? Good." he states. "I'll tell Sol to bring him there. I'll be up in five." The line goes dead.

I push back from the table and head into the bedroom to change.

The closet's lined with order, rows of pressed shirts, dark vests, tailored jackets. I strip, and then slide into a crisp white shirt, a vest, and a jacket falling into place like it's made for me. It is. Power in fabric. I knot the tie tight, then step in front of the mirror.

I straighten my cuffs, slide my holster higher under my jacket. The weight of the gun against my ribs steadies me.

I pass through the living room on my way out, and kiss Lana's forehead as I do, her scent seeping straight into my chest.

"I'll be back soon, sunshine."

I don't look at her, but head to the elevator, enter it and call Sol.

"On my way," he says before I say anything. "Rio updated me."

"Full sweep at the entrance," I say. "He's alone, or he's not coming up. Lock the side stairs. Cameras live, audio live."

"Copy."

The doors open to the club's upper level. The boardroom waits, with a long marble table in black with chairs, black marble walls and one large smoky window overlooking the empty club below.

I move through it; there is a slim drawer under the head seat. I click it open and find the second gun, laid on felt. I close it. The cameras in the corners work. Good.

Rio steps in five minutes later, dressed in his usual attire, a three-piece suit.

"Luciano?" he says.

"Fifteen," I say. "Now ten."

"You left her upstairs?" he asks about Lana.

"Yes."

He nods once, accepting it. "Good."

We settle, one on each flank of the table's head.

My cell buzzes again. Sol: He's here. Alone.

I text back: Frisk him. Take his cell. Then take him up.

A few minutes later, Luciano steps in with Sol on his shoulder. His jacket hangs loose in his hand, shirt open at the collar. Sol's thorough, as always. The tray he sets on the table holds only Luciano's cell. No gun.

"Gentleman," Luciano greets us.

Gentleman?

"Luciano," Rio gives him a mechanical nod from his seat.

I don't stand to greet him. I gesture to a chair. He takes it, and we hear the leather sighing under his weight. Sol hangs back, keeping his distance but never taking his eyes off us.

"You wanted to iron out some shit," I say.

He smiles with only one side of his mouth. "Very well. We can go straight to business."

We stare him down, point-blank.

"I found out about Virgil's cock up." Luciano says. His eyes shift between us, and he finds the camera in the corner without looking at it.

"What cock up?" I ask, flat.

Luciano lifts his brows. "Come on, don't be stupid."

"Try me."

He clicks his tongue, a small scolding. "The missing ten kg of coke."

Rio lets a small smirk take one corner of his mouth, then kills it. "And what's that got to do with us?"

Luciano lifts his hands. "Because the coke you've started to pedal is mine. It's the missing batch. Batches have tells, you should know that boys. I know my product like I know my sins. It's mine."

"Seems like the person you should be crucifying is Virgil." Rio says.

Luciano's eyes don't flicker, but his jaw does. "Virgil is my nephew." He rolls the word in his mouth like it tastes bad. "I don't kill my family. Even if I want to."

"You could delegate," I say.

"I could have asked you, but wait, you already shot him." He waits to see our response, but we don't blink. "Look," he continues. "Let's not waste time. I want to offer you a trade."

"A trade?"

"I'll forgive you the debt of ten kg coke in exchange for the girl Virgil says you have."

"What's with this girl?" Rio asks casually. "Why is she so important?"

"I don't fucking know. But Virgil is a family. And we take care of our own. I'm sure you'd understand. Do we have a deal?"

"No." I say.

"No? Come on, Brox, I'm making this so easy for you. Do you know how much money I'm losing by letting you sell my coke?"

I stand, scraping my chair on the floor. "The girl stays with us."

Rio follows me. "I agree."

Luciano looks between us. "Boys," he says with a tired affection. "You're young. Hungry. It's cute that you want this girl. But you're not stupid."

"We're not," I say.

"Then you know I'm giving you an out," he says. "She's not important to you in the way business is. She's a complication with legs. You hand her over, I forget that my product found your pockets. Everybody walks. Plus, you make money, on top."

"You could forget all you want," Rio says. "Doesn't mean we owe you the courtesy."

"You know what I respect about you boys?" he says, and it's almost conversational now. "You built something fast. You carved a name out of a city that eats names for breakfast. Brick by brick, right?" his smile shows teeth this time. "But every brick needs mortar. You don't get mortar without making enemies into friends sometimes."

"We don't make friends out of threats," I say.

"I'm offering you a deal," he says. "Threats come later."

"She stays," I say. "The debt doesn't exist. If your nephew loses your product, that's a family problem. You want to fix it, start at home. We're not your problem."

Luciano's eyes go flat. "Think twice," he says, and the softness drains. "Because the next time you wake up, you may not find a club down here."

"You're invited to test the locks," Rio says, smiling thin.

Luciano pushes back his chair. He stands without hurry, smooths his jacket, picks up his cell from the tray, glances once at the door, once at me. "You don't know the city yet," he says. "You think you do. You think your names are enough to make people move. But names don't stop fire."

"We don't hide from fire," I say.

"You'd be dangerous in ten years," he nods at us. "It's a shame you're impatient."

He doesn't look back when he leaves. Sol follows him out, and closes the door behind them, and for a long while, no one speaks.

Rio sits first. "Well," he says. "That's a declaration."

A minute of silence passes before Sol reappears.

"He's gone, boss," he mutters, certain.

"Run a sweep on the street, Sol," I order. "Faces we've seen before, faces we haven't. If anyone's parked without paying for the meter, I want their plates in my cell in five minutes.

"On it."

Rio tips his head back, stares at the ceiling.

"He thinks we're smart," I say. "Smart people pick profit over girls."

"Are we smart?" he asks.

"We're young," I chuckle.

He laughs, then looks at me. "Young doesn't mean naive, Brox."

"No," I say. "It means the old hate you for your spine."

Rio drums his fingers once, twice. "Maybe we should do something."

"Mm," I say. "Lunch?"

"Good idea."

The BOARPIT

CHAPTER 15

BROX

I shrug off my jacket and hang it on the stand by the door. Rio does the same, tugging at his tie and rolling his sleeves halfway up his forearms.

Greta's already in the kitchen. We called her from the boardroom on our way up, told her to have lunch ready. She gives us a single nod when she sees us, then she goes straight to the cupboards, pulling out pans and trays without asking a thing. She knows what to cook, what to put out, and how much.

I hear Rio sighing as he drops onto the sofa, stretching an arm across the backrest. I lower myself into the armchair opposite, pulling the gun from my side and setting it on the coffee table.

"I've had enough of the Puccinis," he says. "Enough of Luciano, enough of his mouth. He thinks we're stupid. That we don't understand business?"

My jaw clenches. "It's their mess, their family problem."

From the corner of my eye, I watch Greta laying out dishes on the kitchen counter, our usual place for lunch. Bread in a basket. Olives in a bowl. Then steaming plates of pasta, sauce thick and clinging to the noodles. She finishes with two glasses of white wine, setting them next to the plates.

"Lunch is served." She announces and then she's gone.

Rio sneers as he pushes himself off the sofa first, heading for the kitchen. "Exactly. Luciano's too weak to hold his nephew accountable."

I follow his step and sit across from him. "And now he wants Lana."

His fork scrapes against the plate, the sound deliberate. "Luciano's a threat we can't ignore. We've got to decide how to handle him, before he handles us."

"Yeah, I don't think this ends unless we make it end." I agree.

His eyes narrow. "Then let's end them. We'll get them all in one place. A wedding, a funeral, a birthday celebration, whatever. And we end them all. Every last one."

I sit back and drink my wine. "Poison. They'll choke before they even see it coming."

Rio studies me. "Poison?"

"Cyanide." The choice is too easy. "Fast. Efficient. No second chances."

He stabs at the pasta but doesn't eat. "Cyanide."

I swirl the wine, watching it ripple. "And we make damn sure Virgil's at that table. He doesn't crawl out of this. Not this time."

Rio finally drags a mouthful of pasta onto his fork. "What I can't figure out is how the fuck he knew Lana was here. He didn't just stumble on it, someone told him."

I set the glass down. "Valentino?"

"He wouldn't dare." Rio shoots me a cold look. "It has to be someone who was with Jack Crawford that night."

"Then we find out who. We go back to the office, pull every second of that CCTV on the night in the cinema room club. We trace the leak."

Rio nods. "And when we find out who it is, they'll die–"

"Hey... you're here."

Lana steps into the area between the living room and kitchen, eyes flicking between us. Her hair's loose, falling in soft waves over her shoulders. She's in a beige bodycon dress up to her knees, elegant, simple, like she's stepped straight out of a magazine shoot. Out of place, yet exactly where she should be.

She crosses the space as Rio drags a bar stool out with his shoe, and she sits.

"Is everything okay? How was the meeting with Luciano?" she asks.

Rio glances at me, probably wondering why she knows. I shrug.

"You remember that coke you found for us?" Rio says casually. "The one that belongs to Luciano?"

"Yes." she says, wary now.

"He found out we're selling it. And he said he'll forget about it, if we handed you over."

Her eyes go wide, her lips parting like the words caught her in the throat.

Then Rio leans back, as if he hasn't just set her world on fire. "Hungry?"

"I... yes."

I extend my hand to her. "Don't worry. He's only playing."

She searches my face. "So... that didn't happen?"

"Oh, no, it happened," I say. "Every word. Rio was telling the truth. But we're not giving you up, cupcake. Not just yet."

Her hand slips into mine, soft, steady. I twirl a forkful of pasta, hold it out. "Open."

She obeys. The way her mouth parts, the flick of her tongue when she licks sauce from her lip, Rio and I both watch her like she's the only meal in the room.

"I mean, really," I grin, "who'd look after our pets if you're not here?" I wink at her.

Rio stares at her, then at me.

Her lips curve, a flicker of surprise in her eyes. "Wait... you talked to Rio about it?"

"Talk to me about what?" Rio arches a brow.

I chuckle. "Lana here is very ambitious. Unlike any pet we've ever had."

Rio's lip curls in half amusement, half warning, waiting on more information. "O-kay."

I laugh. "You know what she asked me?"

"What?"

I tip my chin toward her. "Tell him," I say to Lana. Coaxing and commanding her at the same time. "Go on."

"I asked... I wanted to wake up in his room one day. Or yours."

"Or mine?" his brows crook. "What for?"

Her chin lifts. "Every time I fall asleep after we play, I wake up alone in my room. I don't want that anymore. I want... mornings. Coffee. Us."

Rio flicks his gaze to me, then back to her. His laugh is short, edged. "You're bold, I'll give you that."

But Lana isn't finished. "And there's something else."

"Go on."

"You know how hard I work."

"Can't deny that princess." He chuckles.

"I want to be in charge of the pets." Her words cut clean, leaving no room for doubt. Rio stares at her, then at me, and then he lets out a laugh that isn't light at all. "You're insane."

"Ambitious," I correct, my grin widening.

Lana doesn't flinch. "As I said to Brox, I'd fire Dr. Morales first. She's careless." She glances at us. "I'd bring in someone better. I'd set rules. Panic buttons. Limits. Real care."

Rio barks another laugh. "Pets don't need care, they need training."

"Wrong," she says, steady. "The pets are trained already. They now crave the rooms. They want them. That's why they come back. But they need someone to protect them too. Someone who sees them as more than toys."

Rio leans back, arms crossed. His lip curls. "You've got some balls, princess. You think you can run what we built?"

She doesn't blink. "With you. At your side. Yes."

For a beat, silence rules the room. I'm watching Rio, watching Lana, watching the way neither of them breaks eye contact.

"You should've heard her earlier," I say, chuckling. "She even remembered to call me Daddy when she asked."

Rio's expression darkens, then shifts, interest flashing in his eyes despite himself.

Lana swallows, but her gaze never wavers. "I know what I want. And I'm not afraid to say it."

"You do, huh?" Rio's expression darkens as he rests his hand on Lana's thigh. "Stand up, pet."

She slides off her bar stool, still gazing at Rio. Her eyes turn that dark deep green, offering you a place to get lost in.

"Strip, Lana," Rio commands. "Show us what we're working with."

Lana takes a deep breath to steady herself before grasping the hem of her dress. Slowly, she peels it off her body, the fabric rustling as it slides over her hips in a single fluid motion, revealing ample breasts that I often use as a pillow. I'm a vulture when I'm with her. I could drink in every inch of her exposed flesh.

With no bra holding her back, Lana's breasts are bared, nipples hardened and inviting. She continues the sensual performance, shimming out of her panties until they pool around her ankles.

Step by step, she kicks free from the last barrier between us and her nakedness.

Now completely nude before us, Lana stands on display as our eyes roam over every curve of her body.

"Be a good girl and crawl right here under the kitchen counter please," he says. "With your ass right where Brox is." Lana's eyes widen slightly before she gracefully bends down, almost crouching under the kitchen counter, her back meeting the cold underside of the counter. Her head tilts up at Rio, her lips parted and eyes locked with his, and her ass right in front of me.

Rio inhales sharply, welcoming the feeling of what's to come as she leans in toward him. From what I can see, she has unbuttoned his pants, wrapped her fingers around him, and she's taken him into her mouth.

Rio's hands grip the edge of the counter, as he tries to contain himself with a dark smile on his lips. But by now, he is entirely at her mercy, willingly drowning in the pleasure she offers him.

I glance down at Lana's perked ass, and I gently slide my fingers past her entrance, growling as I feel her arousal. Her hips buck in response to the rhythmic motions of my fingers inside her, following with her muffled moans.

I step down from my bar stool and kneel behind her; I'm after tasting her sweet arousal. Without waiting I lap up at her sensitive cunt, her folds, her ass, before going down to her pulsating nub. She writhes with a need for release, as she's taking Rio in throat deep.

"That's it, baby, just like that," I encourage her between nips, and thrusts of my tongue, watching the way she expertly handles Rio. "Now turn around for me, let Rio get a taste of you."

Lana pulls away from Rio and swiftly moves beneath the counter, turning to the other side and right in front of me, showing me a mischievous grin on her flushed face.

I press her lips in a hungry kiss, my hand cradling the side of her face as I devour her mouth. Then I stand up and unbutton my pants, releasing my thick, throbbing cock in front of her face.

Her lips eagerly latch onto my cock, sucking, making me groan and growl in response. Opposite me, I hear Rio's groans as he's sunk to his knees, indulging in every drop of her sweet nectar with his tongue.

Then he rises up, and slides into her cunt from behind, holding her steady with his hands and thrusting in her slowly. I grip her hair firmly and push my cock inside her mouth.

Both Rio and I are standing, the kitchen counter between us still has food on it. I grab the glass of white wine nearby, and Rio does the same. We clink our glasses, and drink to celebrate our little ambitious pet.

Soon, the pumping and bobbing start to gain velocity without us wanting to end it. It's Lana. It's what she does. Rio quickly pulls away. "Come here, Lana," he commands. "Sit here."

She obediently comes out from under the counter, and takes a seat on the bar stool, holding the counter with her hands, as I'm left with a glistening cock that's jutting left and right as I, too, walk over to the other side.

She's perched on the edge of the bar stool, her buttocks curve from behind it and Rio leans over her, and starts with gentle coaxing, stretching her ass inch by inch. The small thrusts of his hips increase in tempo, and judging by his groans, he's fully in.

I'm hungry for a piece of that too. I walk over to her and immediately, he makes a space, we both know there's plenty of Lana to go around. Just after he stretches her, and pumps into her a few times, he pulls out, and it's my turn now. With enough arousal from her cunt, I enter her with ease and start thrusting. Hearing every broken note from her throat, dragged out of her one breath at a time, is what fuels me. I grunt with her, and after nearly reaching my end, I leave her ass gaping, empty, and let Rio have a go. She sings for us, moans, begs as we alternate fucking her ass while her breasts bounce with each thrust.

"Daddy?" she's breathless.

"Yes, baby?" Rio leans down to meet her gaze, his palm landing on her breast as he gives it a sharp slap.

"I need you, Daddy." She's begging.

I shift to the front, and devour her mouth, and then slap her face a few times as she takes my cock with both hands and starts jerking me.

"You want my cum, don't you?" I hold her jaw in my hand.

"Yes, please, Daddy. Yes!" she's pleading with her tongue out.

My other hand is down between her legs, on her pulsating nub. I smear her arousal over it, rubbing it over and over, in tune with her moans, sweet and heavenly and God sent.

I can't last any longer, I growl, fucking tsunami crashes over me and ribbon after ribbon of sperm shoots over her tits and face; and she tries to licks every drop I give her.

Rio's finished too, he's buried inside her, still growling.

And Lana... Lana's flying, she reaches orgasm after orgasm, trembling and releasing high-pitched cries of ecstasy.

Totally spent, she leans on me as Rio pulls out, and I pick her up in my arms. I don't think she can walk after this game.

She looks up at us both with lustful eyes, she's still flying.

"Was I good, Daddies? Was I good enough to take care of your pets?"

"Princess, you're too good!" Rio strokes her hair. "But we'll save this talk for another time."

RIO

What a fucking life Lana offers. One filled with hedonism, lust and orgasms – nonstop. And she's getting more confident. The way she acts, the way she loves her work. Perfection.

Still, I laughed at her request to run the pets. And to wake up with us, too. I'm not sure that's the best idea. Fuck, I can't get her out of my head, and it's been half an hour. My cock is hard again.

Brox and I left Lana in her bedroom to rest; she has too many clients to work with tonight, plus entertaining us after hours. I told Greta to make sure she eats well before she heads out, in case we don't come back on time.

We're on our way to the office to figure out how Virgil found out about Lana being here. We got to sort out the Puccinis once and for all. Because Lana isn't going anywhere. *Finders keepers, motherfucker.*

I pull my jacket back on, and Brox grabs his from the stand, then picks his gun up off the coffee table, sliding it into the holster.

"I'll talk to Dr. Morales about the cyanide." I say as we head for the elevator, our steps in sync.

"Good. We want this done in house." He agrees.

The elevator takes us to our office in less than five minutes.

Brox sits in the chair, with the desk sitting heavy in the middle of the room, screens mounted across the far wall, cables snaking around them. This is the heart of our operation, the eye that watches everything.

I stand next to him and watch him waking up the screens with a few keystrokes.

He pulls up the feed from that night in room one, when Jack Crawford visited, and rewinds until the night spills out again on screen, Jack walking in like he owns the world. Twelve men trailing him, orbiting his weight.

"Freeze there," I say.

Brox taps the keyboard, slowing it frame by frame. The faces sharpen, one after another, the camera catching the details.

We run the facial recognition software, letting the system work through them one at a time. A ping, then another, but nothing worth writing down. Until finally, one Italian name pops on the screen.

Giuseppe Benini.

Retired from the mafia. Supposedly out of the game. But I recognize his face, I've seen him with Luciano before.

"Benini," Brox mutters, leaning forward.

"Has to be the one who talked," I say. It fits too neatly. A man with old ties to the Puccini family. "Virgil was probably asking questions, and he answered, not knowing he's giving away a lot. Which sealed his fate."

Brox doesn't answer right away. He stares at the screen like he can burn through it, then finally glances at me.

"There's our gathering. A funeral."

I grin. "Address?"

He clicks again, pulling up the record. The file unfolds, house, street, tidy neighborhood.

My adrenaline kicks in. "Let's go."

We move to the back wall. It looks ordinary enough, lined with black marble, but Brox presses a hidden panel, and it slides open with a whisper. Behind it, steel racks gleam. Guns, shotguns, extra magazines stacked neat. All the tools we need for a day out.

We don't talk while we load up. I grab a second gun, tuck it into the back of my waistband, then fill my jacket with fresh mags. Brox does the same.

In five minutes, we're moving again, down through the club, and into the garage. The motion lights snap on, and our steps start to echo on the concrete while we reach my Corvette.

Once there, I unlock my car with a click and enter it. Brox settles into the passenger seat and tosses me a glance as he adjusts the cuffs of his three-piece suit.

The city rolls out under us fast, with Miami sunlight bouncing off glass towers. The car eats the road, as the engine growls low, a sound making people look up at us.

On the drive I follow the GPS tracker, ticking us closer, block by block, until we pull onto a quiet street and Giuseppe's house comes into view. A pristine little palace with trimmed garden and spotless driveway.

And there he is. Outside. Gray hair slicked, suit pressed, shoes polished. His wife is there too, they seem to be dressed for some event.

Lucky for us, no's one around.

I pull the Corvette straight into the driveway. The sound makes Giuseppe turn his head, and his smile falters. He knows before he even sees the guns.

We step out, my hand curling around the gun, I've done this too many times. Brox mirrors me.

Giuseppe freezes. His wife clutches his arm, her eyes open wide, her mouth is already open. The scream hasn't come yet, but it's in her throat.

I step close enough that the metal shines in the corner of his vision.

"You should've kept your mouth shut, asshole."

The first shot cracks, then another, until we empty the whole magazine in his body, and then we turn on his wife. Their bodies jerk, fold, and finally collapse, with blood painting the driveway.

Brox and I move together back to the Corvette. We slide into our seats like we just stepped out of a meeting.

I bring the engine to life and roll back onto the street, leaving the neighborhood exactly as we found it, minus two lives.

"As you said, there's our funeral," I say, sliding the gun back into my holster.

Brox smirks.

CHAPTER 16

LANA

Just as I let down my guard, the world flips.

My lungs seize when a big, rough hand clamps over my mouth, the pressure crushing my scream.

Valentino's voice rasps against my cheek. "Not a sound," he hisses. "You won't like what follows."

Before I can struggle, he's whipping lengths of rope around my wrists and ankles. His movements are disturbingly expert, like he's done this a thousand times. He shoves me face-down onto the bed, straps my wrists above me to the headboard, cinches my ankles to the footposts. Pain flares where the ropes bite into my skin.

"Please," I choke out. "Don't–"

He yanks my hair aside, his knuckles cool and deliberate against the nape of my neck.

"No one can hear you," his tone is chilling. "So just stay quiet. It'll be easier."

"Why me?" I yank uselessly at the ropes. "Why–"

He tilts his head. "Virgil still wants you." He gives a small shrug. "Of course, we gonna have some fun before I hand you over."

I shake my head, begging. "Please.. Let me go."

He crouches by the mattress so his eyes are level with mine, unzips a small case and lays it open on the bed beside my hip. I'm still naked from our afternoon games in the kitchen and I can see knives in scabbards, a few serrated, a few not. He chooses one with a saw edge and tests the point against his thumbnail.

The first touch of the blade is light against the back of my bum cheek. He draws it in a shallow line, and I gasp; it burns after the cold. He isn't carving; he's sketching. He pauses to tilt his head and admire the thin red seam.

"Please stop," I sob, tears blurring my vision. "Please–"

He gives me another shallow line, this time on my shoulder blade, it feels like a scratch from a thorn. He hums.

"Lana?" Greta steps in, balancing a tray with food and coffee for me. Her eyes widen and the cup rattles against its saucer.

Valentino stands in the same motion, and now I see a gun in his hand. "Greta. Leave the tray, please."

Greta freezes, her gaze flicking between me and the gun. I crumble in silence, tears pooling at the corners of my vision.

"Please, Greta–" I start.

Greta sets the tray on the dresser, her gaze darting to the door, and it's a split-second decision, but it's enough. Valentino notices. His eyes flare wide, his jaw tightening as if she's just lit a fuse.

"Don't you dare," he snaps.

Greta backs a step, then another. When she turns toward the hallway, he lunges but she manages to escape him. From what I can see, she stumbles towards the dining room, but he follows her fast, with a pointed gun. I strain against the ropes, powerless, with panic in my chest. Then a gunshot breaks the air in half.

I flinch so violently the rope burns my wrists. The sound loops in my head, and I sob.

Valentino returns, his chest still heaving and irritation creasing his brow. "That was not the plan," he mutters to himself, wiping something damp from his trousers. "I liked her."

"You...killed her?" I whisper, disbelief tightens my throat.

He doesn't answer. He sets the gun beside me, lifts a handkerchief from his case, and jams it into my mouth. "This will keep you quiet," he says. "Only for a little while."

I shake my head, the stiff cloth pressing against my lips, stifling my panic. I choke on a sob and swallow it back.

"Shh!" Valentino hisses, panic clawing through his voice.

Outside, metal groans, it's the elevator, I'm sure of it. Rio and Brox's footsteps echo down the hallway.

"With Sol more hands-on, we're covered," Rio says, his words jagged. "We're safe, but we're not taking chances."

"Luciano's got a funeral to get to," Brox answers. "He won't make his move before Giuseppe is in the ground. That buys us days."

They're almost here. My heart hammers so hard it's going to burst from my chest. Valentino's hand trembles around the gun, he's not sure what to do.

And suddenly, the voices vanish, and the footsteps stop.

The doorknob turns, agonizingly slow. The door cracks open an inch, then more. Rio steps in first, Brox behind him, both freezing as their eyes absorb every detail of this room – of us.

Valentino levels the gun at them. His jaw works; a flicker of real terror darkens his eyes.

"I thought they'd take care of you," he stammers. "Virgil said–" his words shrivel on his tongue.

"Drop it," Rio growls. His voice is sharp steel. "Just drop it."

"If you kill me," Rio continues in a whisper that rumbles, "Brox will skin you alive. If you shoot

Brox, you don't want to know what I'd do to you. Either way – today's your last day on earth."

"You always were the best team, you two."

Valentino kneels, places the gun on the floor, then raises his hands. "Sons," he says. "We can–"

"Shut up," Brox says and rushes to my side.

"I can explain. Virgil–" Valentino pleads.

"Don't. Say. His name." Rio's words snap like a whip.

Brox presses his knife under the rope at my ankle. One cut, then another. He pauses at my wrists, tests the knots, slices through. Pain roars back as blood floods my arms and I can't choke down the sound of my own scream.

"I've got you," Brox murmurs, tossing a sheet over me.

I gag the cloth from my mouth with a cough, swallowing past a quake in my throat. The room sways as I haul myself upright on the mattress.

Rio walks up to where I am and kneels. Something breaks across his face when he sees me, fury, relief, it's too fast to name. He cups my chin, tilting my face up so he can see my eyes.

"You're okay?" he asks.

I nod.

"Did he cut you?"

"No."

He nods and moves his gaze dead on Valentino. "Move," he orders, nudging the gun toward him.

"Please," Valentino begs, voice ragged. "It wasn't meant to go like this."

Rio's jaw snaps. "MOVE."

Brox wraps an arm beneath mine. My legs quake, but I rise.

"He's a psycho," I mutter.

Three steps in, and Rio freezes mid-stride. His back muscles twist to stone.

"You killed GRETA??" he bellows.

"For fuck's sake, Valentino. You went too far today." Brox roars.

Valentino's head whips toward the dining room. "I didn't mean it. She walked in and surprised me," his voice shatters on the air. "I liked her."

"You liked her?" Rio repeats, incredulous fury boiling over.

Valentino presses his palms together, as though praying. "I can make it right–"

"No," Rio spits. "You die today."

Valentino's pleas die on his lips as Rio's fury shakes the penthouse walls. "You bastard, you killed GRETA!"

"Come on, let's get you out of here," Brox guides me out of mine and inside his bedroom, and eases me onto the bed's edge. He inspects my wrists carefully, the stings are fierce.

"Motherfucker." he mutters to himself.

BROX

Lana's asleep in my bed. After what had happened to her, I let her stay in tonight. No work, no noise. She didn't want to be alone in my room, but her body gave way, the adrenaline was gone. She curled into my sheets and shut down. First time sleeping in my bed, not her own.

I step into the living room and see Rio sitting in the chair, gun steady in his hand. The barrel's aimed at Valentino.

Valentino is on the sofa. His hands are tied with a zip tie. His eyes flick between Rio and me, measuring us, waiting.

Rio mutters, not looking away from him. "Night off, huh?" he jerks his chin toward my bedroom. "Since when do our pets get a night off?"

I hold his stare. "You gotta be joking, Rio. Don't you think we've got other problems to take care of right now?"

His eyes stay hard on Valentino, his finger rests loose but ready on the trigger. Valentino shifts uneasily on the sofa, his eyes darting to the barrel fixed on him. Rio doesn't move, doesn't blink, he's set on pulling the trigger, I can tell.

Valentino lifts his hands, his palms tremble, desperation leaking into his voice. "I can be useful, Rio. I'll give you anything, anything you want."

"I want you dead. Can you give me that?" Rio shoots back.

"I brought you up, I was there when no one else was, for both of you, please," Valentino's voice shakes. "One chance, that's all I'm asking. Let me prove I can still serve you."

A ping cuts through the air and Valentino flinches, his hand sliding toward his pocket. Rio jumps in and yanks the cell out. Standing above him, he reads the screen, then shows me.

He's got a message from Virgil: Tomorrow we lay Giuseppe and Clara Benini to rest at his home, surrounded by family and close friends. You're welcome to join us at noon.

Rio laughs once, harsh. He slips the cell into his own pocket and looks down at Valentino. "You're one lucky son of a bitch, Valentino!"

"I am?" He's confused.

"I just thought of something you can do for me. That one chance you begged for. I'll give it to you."

His eyes narrow. "Why? What's going on?"

"You've been invited to a funeral tomorrow at noon. They'll bury Giuseppe and his wife."

He swallows, still not following. "I-I didn't know Giuseppe was dead."

"He is. And you'll make sure the rest of them are." Rio states and looks at me. "After the burial, the meal at Giuseppe's house. That's where we'll take the Grappa. It's traditional. And respectful."

"Genius!" I grin.

"Do this, and I'll let you live." Rio meets Valentino's death-black stare, making a deal with the devil. Of course, Valentino is a problem we've tolerated for far too long and we know better than to make deals with him.

Valentino blinks. "What's in the Grappa?"

"Cyanide." Rio locks eyes with him, almost daring him to object.

His throat bobs again, slower this time. "And if I don't want to do it?"

"We have two options if you don't want to do it. Option one is simple, I could kill you right now. And option two, I could remind the police of all the missing bodies in Miami, as many as you can count."

Worry flickers in his eyes.

"You think we don't have leverage?" Rio reminds him. "Hell, you're the one who taught us that."

"Tomorrow at the funeral." I sit opposite Valentino, on the chair, and Rio sits next to him. "You'll take the box of Grappa we'll give you, six bottles in total. You'll say you're sorry for their loss, leave the bottles there, and watch them drink it."

CHAPTER 17

RIO

We put Valentino in the guest room. I don't like calling it a cell, but that's what it is now.

He stands in the doorway, with a split lip. For Greta, he deserves worse. He's lucky we need him for tomorrow.

"Inside," I tell him.

He drags his feet, so I shove him forward. I'm done with his games tonight.

"In the morning, you'll get dressed, and head to Giuseppe's with the Grappa." I state.

He gives me that eerie half-smile of his and says nothing.

I lock the door behind him, but I know I'll sleep better knowing there's a camera tucked in the crown molding.

I walk down the hall, past the wall of glass that faces the city. The reflection throws back my clenched jaw and the scowl carved into my face. I don't correct it.

In the kitchen, the island's clean except for the splattered blood in the corner. I fold the towel over it. Greta would deal with it tomorrow... Shit, my chest tightens when I remember her body is in a bag, by the staircase. Sol will have to move it tonight. Another thing for Sol to do.

I open the fridge and see a half-bottle of water. I take it and sit on the bar stool where I can see the hallway and the door Valentino's behind.

I pull up his cell and go straight to the messages with Virgil.

He's still in the hospital. Good. Hope he dies there. He offered Valentino the deeds to his house, in exchange for Lana. On Luciano's orders. Motherfucker Luciano! I want to smash his cell into the counter until there's nothing but broken glass and plastic shards. The only reason I don't is because we still need him breathing tomorrow. Fucker.

I take another sip of the water. The only reason Lana's still breathing is because we got here in time. My head sketches the other version of tonight – her body on the floor, eyes glassy. The fury in my mind when I picture it is unbearable. I shut it down before it tears me apart.

Valentino will have to be dressed up for tomorrow, and I don't want him to go home for it. Dammit! So I make myself go to my bedroom and from my closet I pick a gray suit that looks better on a dead fish. It's still tailored. It still costs more than most people's rent. I don't care. I fold a white shirt that's not my favorite and a black tie that's too shiny. Then I carry out the outfit and hang it on the knob of Valentino's door.

On the way back I stop outside Brox's room. I knock once and open it.

The room is dimly lit. Brox sits on the edge of the bed, his back to me. Lana's awake, and she's sitting in his lap, her wrists turned up in his hands, he's spreading a cream on her skin, Arnica.

"We're good," I say, my voice low so it doesn't break the room.

Brox finishes massaging her wrists and lays her hands in her lap as Lana's eyes flicker toward me. There's a ring in the whites where tears sat and dried. I lower myself to a knee in front of her.

"Hey princess," I put a strand of her hair behind her ear.

Her gaze drifts to Brox's eyes, and back to me. "Hey."

"How does it feel to finally have a night off?" I want to lighten the mood.

She gives me a sly smile. "I didn't ask for it." Her fingers hook into my lapels, tugging me out of the jacket. "Come on," she murmurs. "Come to bed."

I take off my jacket, put my gun on the nightstand and let her pull me on the bed.

"You too," she says to Brox. He's already changed from his suit to his slacks and a t-shirt, and lies next to her, on the other side.

She's on her back and we're facing her. Her hand falls on my hip, and she pulls me to her. She does the same to Brox.

"This is what I want." She whispers.

I look at her as she's lying with her eyes closed, a smile on her lips, and I begin to slowly untie her robe, allowing her body to appear from under the silk. I hook my leg over hers, the one closer to me, and pull it toward me, opening her up. Brox gets the idea and does the same. She's like a doll between us, and we're going to play with it for the night.

Brox's hand trails up her inner thigh, and I do the same. With my mouth I descend on her breast, and nipple, and judging by her writhing, she's loving my tongue. She arches her back as I bite on her breast, as my hand explore her body as if for the first time. This is a first time, this slow sensual moment. I wonder if it's because I feel guilty she nearly died or because I was waiting for a moment like this to fully enjoy her.

Brox' fingers are already between her thighs, drawing moans out of her. She pulls down Brox's slacks, and frees his stealthy cock from its entrapment, and with her other hand is trying to unzip my pants. I take her hand in mine and ease her off, calming her. Her eyes open, and she looks at me, confused.

"Slow down, Lana."

She frowns, and gives me a tiny tantrum jerk, which makes me unzip my pants immediately. My hard cock springs out, ready for action.

She wraps her hand around my cock, and she's already done that with Brox; she's holding me tight and pumping slow, making me pulse in anticipation. I bite her nipple, and kiss her skin, going up to her neck, peppering with her kisses. Her scent is divine and I want to take it all. I've never done this before. Kissing someone so many times in one go.

What is wrong with me? I glance at Brox, devouring her mouth, he's enjoying being pumped, his hips rocking in sync with her hand as his middle and ring fingers are in her cunt. He slides them inside, takes her arousal and rubs her nub, and that's when she stops everything, hoping to get a release while he rotates and swivels over her heaven. But Brox thrusts his fingers again in her cunt, doing the same move, and now her hips buck with his thrusts.

"Fuck!" I need her cunt, and I crave her taste. "Lana, go on all four for me, baby." I order her and end whatever Brox was doing with her.

Lana pulls back from kissing Brox, smiles at him and shrugs. She turns around and goes on all fours as I go behind her.

"Perk your ass, honey." She raises her ass higher, opening her legs as wide as possible. "Good girl. That's good. More if you can."

Brox doesn't get up, he just slides under her and gets to her tits, bouncing freely, looking plentiful and perfect. He grabs them in his hands, and straight, he sets both of them, in his mouth. She moans as I grab her below her butt cheeks and open her up, her cunt and ass now in my face, glistening with the elixir of life.

She writhes under my touch, she wants me to start eating her but I just want to watch her one moment longer. She is perfection I cannot get enough of.

"P-please Daddy...."

Brox's mouth finds her, and I hear him whispering to her. "Shh... Good things come to those who wait."

This is my sign to dig in, I lean down, my tongue lapping at her swollen cunt, her nub, and her ass. Lana's cries fill the room, her body trembling under my touch. I hold her butt cheeks firmly open, keeping her in place as I thrust with my tongue and she bucks downward against it, moaning.

Brox is playing with her nipples, I hear him slapping her tits, as they bounce. I want to drink her up fully, and I do, and when I think I haven't left a drop of her mead, I push two fingers inside her. Her thighs begin to tremble and she treats us to a whimper that becomes one long moan. "D-daddy!" she coats my hand with her juice.

This is heavenly.

I spread her knees wider on the bed, and slide three fingers into her cunt now, take her arousal and smear it over her ass. The way her body is vibrating I want to use her like she deserves.

I push a finger over her ass and the whore that she is, she bucks against it, and I'm in.

I glance at Brox, he's sucking on her tits, and fisting his cock.

"Daddy, f-fuck me," she looks back at me, and jerks into my fingers.

I brush my cock against her arousal, going up and down her cunt, and ease myself into her, but it's going slow. Inch by inch I gain traction and I begin to stretch her out. Fuck! That's fucking too much pleasure as I enter her.

"Thaaa's it, my little pet. Yeess…"

She oozes arousal, now dripping down her leg while she adjusts to my girth, accommodating me and adapting to my rule. I have never taken her or anyone this slow, and the feeling is overwhelming. Unknown to me.

"I want you, Daddy." Her gaze slow and weighted as she's looking back at me. "Inside me, Daddy."

Brox slides his head between her legs and his tongue starts making wonders around and on her clit. Lana's just become an open and willing participant, bouncing into his tongue as I begin to slam into her, relentlessly, to the hilt.

And she doesn't waste a moment, as she reaches for Brox's cock, making him move his body where her mouth is and she leans down on him, bobs her head, starting to suck him. I see his fingers tangling in her hair, and he takes over, he's fucking her mouth, as I ram her ass from behind.

Every sound she makes is proof she belongs here, with us. That's what tips me over, and Brox, I think. She's over the edge too, her muscles clamp down on me, her orgasm tearing through me like lightning, taking me with her.

My pace quickens, my grunts change into a growl, a loud growl and my spawn shoots deep inside her ass, and Brox stills her head on him, shooting at the back of her throat with each jerk of his body.

Spent and panting, the three of us collapse on the bed, our tangled bodies ending up wherever we lay.

Lana is the first to fall asleep, I hear it by the sound she makes when she breathes. Slow, soft, sighing when she moves.

I would do nothing else but stay in bed with her, but I can't sleep. Not now when we're so close to killing the Puccini family.

I get off the bed slowly, trying not to disturb Lana when Brox lifts his head.

"I'll be back." I mouth. I zip up my pants and take my gun from the nightstand.

I step out and close the door behind me. I don't go far. First to the kitchen, to grab a bottle of water, and then back to the hall. I lean against the wall opposite Brox's bedroom and slide down until I'm sitting on the floor, my gun on my thigh, my hand over the grip. I watch the red dot blink above Valentino's door. I watch the hall where the elevator is. I listen for the sound of Lana's breath on the other side of the door. I hear Brox murmur something I can't make out.

Minutes pass. It could be an hour. It could be ten. My cell buzzes once. It's Sol: We bought six boxes of Grappa, in cash. I'll take them to Dr. Morales. Will bring them as soon as they're ready.

Sol is rising to the position of Head of Security. Not only that he keeps everyone safe in the club, but he manages the operations of the coke dealing and now, at such short notice, the cyanide.

I get back to Brox's room as quietly as possible, but he still looks up. His arm is under Lana's neck and the other wrapped around her waist. She's almost on top of him, breathing on his neck, her leg draped over his body.

I step in enough to set a bottle of water on his nightstand, and then step back.

"Sleep," I say. "Four hours. I'll sit in the hall."

He shakes his head once. "We'll switch in two."

We won't, but I don't argue.

BROX

I blink into the morning and realize I'm still on my side, on half of my own pillow. Still in my t-shirt and slacks. Lana's warm back is tucked into my chest. Rio's on the other side of her, his arm is slung over her waist, his hand resting just under my ribs.

I stretch, and that's when I sense my jutting protrusion from my slacks, I could easily kill someone with how hard I am in the morning. I press a kiss on the crown of Lana's head. "Come on, pet," I murmur, voice rough. "Let's make a god use of you today."

Lana makes a soft sound, half in protest, as I lift her head, and take her where she's needed. She moves unhurriedly, as I pull down my slacks, showing her the morning chore.

She puts my cock in her mouth, silently, and then what follows are slow moans she's getting awaken to, and us. There's no argument. She massages my balls, licks my cock like a lollipop, and then twists it with her hand as she bobs her head on me.

"Fuuuck…. You're the perfect object for any home." The sounds spilling from her are like unanswered prayers.

"I know, Daddy." She talks between sucking.

"We'll sell this service daily to our punters."

She moans, and sits up on her knees, she likes that. Her ass in the air, humping as she sucks my morning wood throat deep.

Rio cracks one eye, squints at me, then at her. "More is coming your way, princes," he mutters, the lazy grin showing. He stretches like a bear.

"Yes, Daddy." She glances at him, smiles and continues bobbing on my cock as she starts rubbing Rio through his pants. He hasn't changed last night, too. Probably stayed late, following up on work.

Rio lies on his back next to me and unzips his pants, pulling them down, making space for Lana.

She's kneeling between us, each of her knees between our legs on the bed, she's positioned herself symmetrically perfect in the middle.

She bobs her head on him, and then me, and I'm so close to spraying her with my cum, that I don't want to share her just yet. I take a fistful of her hair and pull her on me. Our eyes lock as my cock enters her mouth, deep, and the moment my glans touches the back of her throat her eyes close. I push her down, as deep as she can until I hear those gurgling sounds, carved from her throat just for me. She hasn't forgotten Rio and she pumps him as she's choking on me, that's our good girl, she always tries to please us both.

"Eyes on me," I hiss.

She bobs her head, throat-deep each time as she's staring at me with that abandon look in her eyes, moaning sweetly just like she's eating a cake. The sounds tearing out of her undo me. I quicken the pace, my grunts turning into one growl, until I shoot hot cum down the back of her throat. She swallows every last drop of me. Good girl.

Without waiting for one moment, she turns to Rio and continues her morning workout.

"Yeeees, my little morning pet." Rio is fully engaged with her deft tongue. "Thaaaat's it."

I chuckle and get out of bed. I can start the day now.

Shower first. I leave them to each other and walk to my ensuite. The shower is one that I welcome, but it makes me think of Lana again and my cock gets hard. I won't be able to leave the penthouse if I keep thinking of her.

I towel off and walk back in the room, to the wardrobe. Three-piece, white shirt, black tie. I pull on the vest, button by button, and watch myself settle in the mirror.

I glance back at Rio and Lana before I step out and see a sight I want to remember for the day. Rio is lying on his back, and Lana is naked, in a reverse cowgirl pose, riding him slowly. Her face turned at the ceiling, hair falling freely on her back as she rides him to the sunrise. Fuck!

The penthouse is quiet when I step into the hall. In the kitchen, there is a box sitting on the counter, neat as a gift. Six bottles, dark glass, wax at the necks. The label looks good, it's imported, the kind of bottle you bring to a man's funeral for sure. I lift one bottle just enough to look at it in the light.

I don't open it. I don't need to. Sol and Dr. Morales already did what we needed to do. Looks great. That's the point.

Coffee. I reach for instinct that isn't there. I don't know how we'll find anyone to work in Greta's place. The coffee machine sits in the corner like a car I never drive. I wipe the dust with my palm, fill the reservoir, fumble with the first pod, then get it right on the second. The noise it makes is too polite for this house. Still, the smell pulls the room together. I line up three cups and let the machine spit life into them one at a time.

Two cups in hand, I head back to my bedroom. The door's ajar. Rio's palm is on the back of Lana's neck, he's devouring her mouth. It looks like they're both feeding off each other's need. She swallows her moan as he moves down her neck and starts to bite and suck her collarbone.

They look up when my shadow touches them.

"Morning, again." I set the cups on the side table. "I thought you'd want coffee."

"Not just yet," Rio chuckles.

I leave my bedroom and close the door behind me, leaving them a little time for themselves.

Looking at the time, Valentino is on my list to wake up next. It's almost eleven o'clock. His door has a suit hooked on the knob. I see it now, he has to be dressed for the funeral, and we wouldn't want him to go anywhere but the funeral. I take the suit with me and unlock the door. Then I cross the floor and kick the foot of the bed. "Wake up."

He flinches hard, then finds me.

"It's late," I say, cutting the zip tie at his wrists with the blade I keep in my pocket. He rubs at the marks.

"Get dressed."

He sits up and grabs the shirt first. He stinks of night sweat and stale fear. He buttons it wrong, unbuttons, then fixes it. Once on, the suit is a tad bigger, but no one expects him to have perfectly fitted clothes. He stands, shrugs into the jacket, then bends to pick up his shoes. He gives me one quick look.

"Can I get a coffee?"

I turn and head to the kitchen, knowing perfectly well he'll follow me. I add another pod in the coffee machine and wait for it to stop hissing.

"Thanks," he says. He doesn't pick up the cup until I've stepped back.

He drinks and sets the cup down.

"I want you to be among the first ones there," I say. "You pay your respects by giving them the box. When enough bodies are in the room, you make yourself useful. Offer to pour."

He nods, "They usually use a tray."

"I know. Pour in the shot glasses. Those are drunk at the same time, in one go."

"When do I leave?"

I meet his eyes so there's no room for misunderstanding. "When you know the job's done."

"And where do I go after?"

"Home," I say. "And wait."

"For–"

"For us."

He takes that in the way a dog takes a command, "You'll... you'll let me know if–"

"If you did your part." I don't put a bow on it. Reward is not a language we speak often because it makes men think they can ask for it.

We walk to the kitchen counter, where the box is. I close the flap and press the cardboard seam flat with my palm.

I hear footsteps behind us, then Rio's voice.

"It's time you head out," he says to Valentino. He has a towel wrapped around his waist, his hair is still wet, and Lana trails him by a step, dressed in one of my shirts. She's got coffee in her hand.

Valentino doesn't look at Rio directly. "Yeah, I'm leaving now."

Rio moves closer until he's a breath away from him. Hate rides on his face. "Open your mouth at the wrong time and I'll close it for good."

Valentino licks his lip again. "I know what to do."

I push the box into Valentino's hands. He grips it right, tucks it against his hip.

He turns, walks for the door, and the elevator. And then we hear the elevator chime and take him away.

Rio leans against the counter and inserts a pod into the coffee machine. After it's made, he tastes it, grimaces, and drinks again, anyway. "Fucking hell, I miss Greta already."

CHAPTER 18

RIO

Once Valentino was out of the door, Brox and I went straight downstairs, to the Boarpit, and buried ourselves in work. Six hours deep. We left Lana at the penthouse with instructions to pamper herself. I told her to prepare for twice the work tonight. She smiled and her eyes gleamed that spark she has only when you tell her she's going to be used.

We're preparing because we're not sure if the Puccinis will come at us with all their might or, if our plan works, try to lick our shoes and join us. Either way, the floor's getting washed in something.

Sol stalks the main floor like a war dog, flanked by two of his hires. Cameras show me everything, the bar flash, the Black Chamber, the corridor that swallows rich men whole and sends them back out shinier and emptier. I've been on comms half the time, on the cell the other half, making sure every exit is manned and every car that slows at the curb gets a good look at. I even called the chief of police, told him to have eyes on our door tonight. He's been using the benefits of the Black Chamber before, so he's always happy to help.

My cell buzzes in my pocket. A text from Sol: Come to my office. Now. Bring Brox.

I look down through the dark-glass and catch him looking up at me, shoving a hand in the air in a tight, panicked wave that says move.

I text Brox: Meet me in Sol's office. He's got something.

Sol's office is adjacent to the bar, a small space enough for two desks, it's where he works from.

I spot Diego wiping down the bar, setting it for the night ahead, just as Brox emerges from the Black Chamber and makes his way over. I take the steel staircase down, the stairs ringing under my shoes.

Sol's office door hangs open, his face white as chalk, one hand frozen toward the TV on the wall like he's pointing at live explosives.

"What," I growl, even as my eyes find the anchor on screen.

"...shocked mourners at the funeral of Giuseppe and Clara Benini were caught in a mass poisoning late this afternoon," the woman is saying. "Twenty-four members and associates of the Puccini crime family are confirmed dead. Investigators believe cyanide was introduced into bottles of grappa served at the wake..."

"Twenty-four?" The laugh tears out of me before I can catch it. "Twenty-four? Yes!"

I clap Brox's shoulder hard. He's already grinning in a silent roar. We smack palms like we just scored the winner. For one hot second the office feels light, like oxygen finally reached it.

"Yes." He drags a palm down his face, half-laugh, half-war cry. "Yes, yes, twenty-four rats dead. We own Miami, you hear me? We–"

"Listen," Sol snaps, voice cracking. "Brox, shut up and listen."

Brox and I turn. The text at the bottom of the screen flips: FUNERAL MASSACRE. POSSIBLE RETALIATION. The anchor's voice flattens to that sober theater they practice in mirrors.

"...police also confirmed a man was found shot dead, execution-style, with a single bullet to the forehead. And we hear now that a young woman was found bound and gagged on the dining table during the funeral, barely alive at the scene. Sources describe an illicit 'auction' interrupted by the poisoning. One photo we're able to air shows the victim being wheeled out by EMTs. We have blurred her face due to the graphic nature of her injuries..."

The image hits me like a fist. She's wrapped in a sheet, her blonde hair, matted dark at the temple. The stretcher slides between suits and uniforms. There's only one problem with the blur, I don't need a face to know a body.

"Again," I growl. "Run that again."

Sol doesn't wait; he's already rewinding on mute. The camera flashes wash through the room a second time. The sheet lifts in the wind. A strand of wet hair catches the light. That mouth. That jaw.

Lana.

Brox stops breathing. I can hear it.

The sound comes back, the reporter's in the field now, hair perfect in the blue light of police beacons. "– what sources describe is that the victim, I quote, "was passed from one man to another, submitting to their every desire. Luciano Puccini, patriarch of the Puccini family, was watching her sadistic degradation, taking bets on how long she can last before her resolve breaks." That happened apparently before all of them saluted with the Grappa, which the authorities presume was spiked with poison..."

My vision shears sideways. When it settles, I'm still standing. I wish I wasn't.

The reporter keeps talking, and the TV shows bodies being wheeled out. On one of them, I recognize my suit. This body has blood on it. Stupid asshole. It must have been Valentino who was executed when he took Lana there. Did he really think Luciano would give him the deeds to his house?

"We left her upstairs." Brox's hand grips the back of a chair. "How the hell she ended up there, Rio?"

"Valentino," my jaw clenches. He's the only one besides us who knows how to get into the penthouse. Something cold unfurls at the base of my skull.

"We're not going to the hospital," Sol says quickly, reading me too well. "They'll be waiting for whoever comes to claim her."

"You think I'm scared of a hospital?" I growl. The TV keeps talking. I don't care. I've got the only words I need. Mercy General.

Brox paces like a caged animal. His eyes keep hooking back to the screen as if he can make it show him a different ending.

"We take the nurse route," he says. "We've done it before. Whites, masks, a bed that isn't a bed. We wheel her out with a chart nobody reads."

"Or we don't," Sol counters. "Too many cameras. The second our faces hit a lens, they become evidence. And if she's tagged as a witness to a massacre? They'll bury her where light can't find her. Different wings. Different rules. You want to take that swing and miss?"

"Let's start from the only thing that matters," I say. "If she talks, what happens?"

Sol swallows. "We become an official investigation, not a rumor. The Black Chamber becomes evidence. Every client we have will quit on us. Our friends start deleting our numbers."

I look at Sol. "Change the whole system tonight at the penthouse. New cards. New logs."

Sol nods once, then twice, already typing on his cell.

My cell buzzes in my pocket. I pull it out, it's an unknown number. I don't like unknowns. I answer, anyway.

Nothing. Just breath.

"Say something," I tell the silence.

A voice comes through that isn't a voice yet, wrecked, sanded raw, the vowels chewed. "Rio."

Everything in me stops.

"Lana," I say. I don't let my face move, but both men in the office catch it, anyway. "Are you okay?"

"No," she whispers, and then breaks into a sob. "They're asking me questions."

"Don't answer them," I say. "Say your lawyer told you not to speak."

"I-I don't have a lawyer." She sniffles. "Do I?"

"You do," I say. "He's on his way. Until he gets there, you say nothing. You understand me? Not one word."

There's a pause. "O-okay," she says, so small I almost miss it. Then, softer. "Are you coming?"

"Soon," I say. "Keep the cell on you."

"It's not mine," she says, and the line goes dead before I can say anything.

I stare at the screen and see my own face reflected back in it.

"What did she say?" Brox asks.

"She's awake," I answer. "And she's scared."

LANA

I'm the first to stir, even though I'm cocooned between them. Warmth presses me from both sides, Brox's weight heavy and grounding, Rio's touch familiar, teasing even in sleep. When I blink my eyes open, I'm met with Brox's gaze, soft, almost tender, though his voice is rough from the night.

"Good morning, beautiful."

His arm tightens around my waist, anchoring me. On the other side, Rio chuckles, his fingers already tracing lazy circles over my nipple, sending sparks through me before I've even spoken.

"Good morning indeed," he says, voice low, playful. "I hope you slept well."

I smile because I did. Better than I have in months, maybe years.

"Like a baby," I admit, threading my fingers through Rio's hair, pulling him just close enough to feel his warmth against me. "And I have you both to thank for that."

"Don't get too comfortable though," Brox murmurs, his eyes cut to Rio.

"You got to be useful for us to keep you."

The words should sting. But instead, they root me deeper, because I know he means them, and still, he holds me close.

Rio leans in, brushing his lips against my cheek, his voice husky in a way that makes my body respond before I even understand it. "I can't wait to parade you in front of all my clients. My cock twitches just thinking about it."

Heat floods me, with something I never imagined I'd find here, two men who shouldn't want me the way they do.

"Being with you both like this... it feels right." I whisper, looking from Rio to Brox. "Thank you."

Brox brushes a strand of hair from my face, his smile morphing into something strange, someone I don't know.

"She's awake!"

I'm confused, and I open my eyes slowly, it's too bright and everything aches. I'm not in the club. I'm not in the penthouse. I'm not in a coffin, too.

I hear a machine to my right that keeps time with me, I look at it and see a clear bag hanging from a metal arm, a line running down into the back of my hand. I try to move my fingers and the tape pulls.

"Can you hear me?" voices blur in and out.

There are nurses around me, a man who says he's a detective. They ask me what's my name.

A woman steps into my view. She doesn't reach for me. She doesn't loom.

"I'm Freeda Charles," she says. "Special Victims Unit. I'm here to make this easier, if I can."

Special Victims Unit. The words rattle and settle. A memory flashes; someone's hand on the back of my neck, the murmur of men, the smell of the varnished wood of a table, a sudden chorus of bodies lining up behind me. Sirens. Hands. A uniformed officer keep asking me if I'm okay. I'm not sure if I was saved or if I just fell into a different mouth.

"Can I get you water?" Freeda says.

I nod. She passes me a cup with a straw, and I sip slowly. I remember being hit on my face. The pain pulses.

"There are a lot of people who want to talk to you," she says. "But you're allowed to rest. You're allowed to say no."

Allowed. The word floats in the room like a balloon.

"I don't..." I rasp. "I don't know where I am."

"Mercy General," Freeda says. "We found you in Giuseppe Benini's house. Do you know him?"

I shake my head.

"Do you want to call someone?" she asks. "A friend. Family."

Family, I wish. Friends? I doubt they see me as their friend. But my mouth forms a name, anyway, like a reflex. "Rio."

Freeda doesn't flinch. "Okay," she says. "Do you have his number?"

I open my hand and wait for her to give me her cell. Freeda holds the cell and deliberates for a split of a second. Then she lays it in my palm.

I know Rio's number by heart. Brox's too. I have no one else to call. I punch in the number, and the cell rings. I'm not sure if I want it to connect. Then it does.

"Yeah."

I remember, this is the second time that I've been ambushed in their penthouse.

"Hello?" he says again. "Say something!"

I latch onto the command out of habit.

"Rio," I whisper.

There's deadly silence, and then his breath has a hitch that betrays him. "Lana. Are you okay?"

Okay. Am I okay? He's never asked me that and meant it like a question, like a concern, not a test.

"No." My eyes well up, immediately, stupidly. I brush my cheek and still end up with salt on my lips. "They're asking me questions." I can't hold up, the lump in my throat is too suffocating, and I start sobbing.

"Don't answer them. Say your lawyer told you not to speak."

"I don't have a lawyer," I sob. "D-do I?"

"You do," he says, immediate, like it was always true. "He's on his way. Until he gets there, you say nothing. You understand me? Not one word."

Not one word.

I want to believe him because that's how I've survived, choose a voice, obey it, become small enough to fit inside someone else's rules.

"O-okay." I exhale. "Are you coming?" I hear the need in my voice and hate myself a little.

"Soon," he says. Soon is a gun with the safety off. Soon means today, tomorrow, next year.

"Keep the cell on you."

"It's not mine," I manage to say before Freeda takes it away from me and hangs up. She slides it back into her pocket. "When you're ready," she says, "I'd like to know your name."

My name. The one attached to all the rooms I couldn't leave. To the pair of hands that taught me everything about pleasure, and to the air that I crave like drugs.

I look at her.

"Georgina," I say. The syllables surprise me. They taste round. New. "Rosario."

I used to go to school with Georgina Rosario. We're the same age, same height, similar looking. And she's been gone from the face of this earth in the last two years. Just like me.

Freeda nods. She writes it without judgment. "Okay, Georgina. Do you know your birthday?"

I shake my head. "I don't remember," I say. "I-I think I was studying. Or I wanted to. Medicine."

Something loosens in my chest when I say it. Medicine. A life that never was.

"Who was that on the call?" she asks.

"A friend." I say quietly. I shouldn't say anything else, Rio ordered.

"Do they have a name?"

I shake my head.

Freeda's eyes soften. "All right. We don't have to figure everything out today. Do you consent to a forensic exam?" she says it quietly. "We can collect evidence in case you choose to report. If you don't want to, we won't. You're in control."

Control. For years it meant the opposite of what it should.

"No," I say. My voice grows a spine.

"Okay." She squeezes my hand. "Let's get you something to eat then. Okay?"

I nod.

Freeda returns with a tray of pasta and orange juice. She speaks briefly to someone at the door before entering by herself.

"They want to ask you questions," Freeda says. "I told them you're not ready to make a statement."

I don't say a word. Instead, I start eating.

"I can get you a victim advocate," Freeda continues. "Separate from me. Someone who can sit with you for interviews, help with paperwork, safety planning. We have a safe house we use for cases like this. Short-term or long-term. No questions. Your decision."

"Do you believe me?" I ask. "If I say I don't remember. Before."

"I believe what you tell me," Freeda says. "And if you don't want to tell me, I believe that too."

"It's just..." My words tangle. "No one good is coming for me..."

I close my eyes. Behind my lids, the club's black walls breathe, the Black Chamber with its alluring soft music and the air that clings to my skin like a second mouth. Rio and Brox, I love them in the way a flame loves a wick. I can pretend I don't. It would be easier.

If I stay, my obsession with what they give me eats my horizon. If I run, my future chews theirs to bone. The math doesn't work, either way.

"I don't want to go back," I say. It's the first time I say it out loud. The room doesn't change. The ceiling holds. The machine keeps time. I'm the only thing that moves.

"All right," Freeda says, like that's a possible thing, like I'm not marking myself for death. "Then we'll plan for that."

"How?" my voice cracks on the word.

"Step by step. We start with today. We assign you a case number without your name. We get you to a place where people who mean you harm can't find you. We keep your location locked. We connect you with a counsellor if you want one. We talk about what you want to do next. School. Work. Sleep."

"School," I say before fear can make me take it back. "I... I think I was good at it. I think I could be again."

"Then we put that in the plan," she says. "I know people who know people who fund second chances. You won't be the first. Or the last."

Second chances. The blanket's heat has soaked into me. A strange, shy animal opens one eye in my chest. Hope is an ugly little thing when it's new. It blinks in the light.

"Okay," I say. "Okay."

Two weeks is a lifetime in a safe house. The building is anonymous from the street, nothing in a row of nothings. Inside, there are soft chairs and too many women who know how to talk without telling you anything. In the mornings, someone makes coffee that tastes better than it's supposed to. I learn when the washing machines are free. I learn how to sleep with a chair propped under the door handle and then, slowly, without it.

Freeda visits twice a week, sometimes three. She never arrives empty-handed. The first time she brings a stack of forms for me, the second, she brings a notebook with a hard blue cover. "For when you remember things," she says. "Or for when you don't and want to write, anyway."

I write the dates on the first page but not the year. On the second page I write words that feel like me and see which ones stay. Pulse. Passion. Coffee. Fear. Blue. I write the name Georgina ten times until it looks like it belongs to my hand.

No one calls me Lana here. No one sends me 'down to work'. I miss that. The part I was addicted to. No one calls me pet or sunshine or good girl. No one orders me to open my mouth, and I open it, anyway, when I want to, to say normal things like pass the salt and does this bus go downtown and can I sit here.

Freeda gave me a cell, and for the first three days I stare at it like a dog looks at a door. By day four I move it into the drawer. By day six I half-dream it ringing and wake up with my heart stamping through my chest. By day nine the dreams slow. By day eleven I memorize Freeda's number instead, because that's a rope I can climb.

Some nights I miss Rio and Brox so much I taste metal again. The missing is chemical, like withdrawal, like my body got used to a dosage of them and I'm sweating it out. I lie on the mattress in the safe house room, stare at the ceiling and repeat the words Freeda gave me 'You're allowed not to go back.'

In the afternoons, I walk to the library with my head down. I pick a corner table and I read. Anatomy first, because the lines of the body make sense when nothing else does. Vascular pathways. The quiet logic of the heart pushing and pushing. Then basic Chem, because white on white still haunts me, powder into powder, how something pure gets stepped on until it looks the same. I learn the names again so they can't trick me anymore. Sodium bicarbonate. Levamisole. Lidocaine. Words that feel like handles on doors.

Freeda keeps her promises. One visit, she brings a flyer with the corner folded down. "Small scholarship," she says. "Bridge program. People who paused school and want to restart. The application isn't... friendly. But we can make it speak your language."

"I don't have transcripts," I say, panic pricking. "I don't have anything."

"We'll say you're rebuilding," she says. "We'll say it's not a lack, it's a plan."

"Is that allowed?"

"You're allowed to shape your story," she says.

That night I dream of the Boarpit. The Black Chamber breathes again. In the dream I'm not afraid. I'm standing in the doorway, Rio watches me and doesn't reach. In the dream, Brox smiles and steps back, palms up, like surrender.

I wake before the ending. The room is quiet. The chair is not under the door. I make coffee in the kitchenette and drink it.

I take the notebook and hold it against my sternum like a shield.

What if they come? Rio said they will.

I take a long breath. It stretches my ribs and for a second, my body feels like a house the right size for me. There's grief in the corners, sure. There's fear in the closet. But there's also a room with a desk. There's also a stack of books and a calendar with days I get to write in pen.

I turn to a clean page and write the date at the top. Then I write my name, the one I'm holding for now, and below it, in smaller letters, the one that still aches in my mouth, in case I need to remember that I once belonged to something that wanted to keep me.

Georgina Rosario.

Lana Rayne.

I draw a line between them with the pen.
Not a wall. A bridge. Definitely a bridge.

The story continues in

Book 2 of the Miami Ruthless series:

RIO BOAR

The BOARPIT

314

ALSO BY ALEXANDRA IFF

If you're after a super spicy reverse harem dark mafia romance with a unique plot, you can find the New York Mafia Vengeance series on Amazon and Kindle Unlimited.

ORION Ruined
LOGAN Punished
KAI Tortured
MAISY the SLAV

Read about the London's hottest BDSM couple, Alexander and Amelia in Collar OF Freedom series on Amazon. FREE in Kindle Unlimited.

The Collar of Freedom
The Collar of Sacrifice
The Collar of Redemption

If you enjoy super spicy short stories, Alexandra also writes the Flash Burn series feat James and Eva.

Books 1, 2, 3 and 4 are available now.

Flash Burn I
Flash Burn II
Flash Burn III
Flash Burn IV

If you're curious about New York's most captivating couple, Dmitri and Trinity, and their daring diamond heist, you can dive into Alexandra's standalone novel, More Than Just A Pair Of Pumps, available now on Amazon.

FREE with Kindle Unlimited.

More Than Just A Pair Of Pumps

ABOUT THE AUTHOR

Alexandra is a dark romance author who writes sinfully addictive stories where brutal alpha males meet fierce, no-bullshit women who give as good as they get (eventually, of course!).

Join Alexandra's reader group for the latest news, book recommendation and plenty of fun.

https://www.facebook.com/groups/alexandraiff

Get sneak peeks and spicy snippets from her up and coming books, plus exclusive news about future releases, giveaways, and other fun stuff, by signing up to her mailing list at

www.alexandraiff.com